143

By
Jade Winters

Also by Jade Winters

Novellas

Talk Me Down From The Edge

Short stories

The Makeover
Love on the Cards
The Love Letter
Temptation

For Ali
Thank you for giving me the key to my chains

CHAPTER 1

THE TENTH FLOOR of the Parliament View apartment block overlooked the city of London. The living room's floor-to-ceiling windows offered panoramic views of the River Thames, upon which the illuminated Houses of Parliament sat, highlighting its striking architecture. Like most days, Rebecca awoke ahead of her five-thirty a.m. alarm call and stood at the window of her apartment watching London come alive. It was hard not to be in awe of the city from this angle — most people only saw London from the ground upwards. She loved the beauty and history that epitomised the city. For a few more moments she watched the road below her, alive with braided strands of traffic, then walked back over to the bed and gently lowered herself down, being careful not to wake its sleeping occupant.

Rebecca never tired of looking at Genevieve while she slept. Every morning she drank in the beautiful oval-shaped face framed with blonde highlighted dark brown hair, the barely noticeable little scar just above her top lip — the result of a childhood accident — and the small mole on her right cheek that only enhanced her beauty. Genevieve stirred and opened her sleepy eyes.

"Hey you," she said, a broad lazy grin lighting up her face.

"Hey yourself," Rebecca replied with a smile,

leaning over and covering Genevieve's face with little kisses before drawing back to look directly into deep green eyes. "I love you."

"How much?" Genevieve looked mischievous.

"I can't quite think of a word that describes it accurately."

"So I'll never know..."

"Oh, I think I can find another way until the word comes to mind!" Rebecca said as they dived under the quilt laughing.

Much later they lay breathless, their bodies entwined with one another, not speaking, just being. Their lovemaking had always evoked a form of contentment. They had not been cursed with the dreaded "lesbian bed death" that a lot of their lesbian friends had been through. They were attracted to each other now as much as they had been when they'd first met. Though it was not with the same urgency, their lovemaking was still intense. Genevieve was the first one to reluctantly move out of their embrace.

"Why do we always end up having sex before we go to work? It just makes me want to stay in bed with you all day." She sat up looking down at Rebecca, who was now stretching on her back.

"But just think: We have the whole weekend to do nothing but please ourselves... and each other," Rebecca said languorously, winking at Genevieve. "Now please, cover that body before we really do end up not leaving the bed!"

With both women finally dressed and at the kitchen table eating breakfast, the subject of the evening's event arose.

"Are you sure you don't mind me going to Paul's

show tonight?" Genevieve said as she sipped her freshly squeezed orange juice.

"Positive," Rebecca replied, with more conviction than she felt. "What's he going to do — ravish you over his paintings? Come to think of it, I wouldn't put it past him." She popped the last remains of her croissant into her mouth and rose quickly, starting to clear the table.

Genevieve smiled.

"You know something? I think I want to marry you," she said, changing the subject. She decided it might be better if, for now at least, she avoided the issue of Paul's sudden invitation for her to attend his show that evening.

"Let's not even go there with that one," Rebecca said, leaning over and dropping a kiss on Genevieve's forehead. She loaded the dishwasher and turned to see Genevieve looking at her with mock surprise.

"What?" she asked innocently, stifling a smile as she imagined walking down the aisle with Genevieve. Rebecca and Genevieve often spoke about a civil partnership, but neither of them could seriously go through with it. They had both agreed they would die of embarrassment, so it was better to stay as they were. Their property was to be left to the surviving partner, so as far as they were concerned, they had the important areas covered and they didn't need to publicly declare their love for each other to know they were committed for life. Rebecca had all she wanted: A woman that she loved more than life itself and a job as a freelance art critic, which had been more of a passion than a career for the past six years.

According to Rebecca, art critics fell into different

groups. There were the highbrow critics who wrote for art journals and whose targeted audience was assumed to be quite knowledgeable about the arts and understood the everyday jargon that was used. Then there were those who wrote for the daily or weekly newspapers, whose targeted audience didn't know their arse from their elbow, and thus the critic wrote in a more informal way, telling the masses of their subjective view on the piece they were writing about. Rebecca, on the other hand, was more interested in informing the public of what the artist was trying to get across, rather than give her own subjective views. It was because of this that she was one of London's most successful art critics.

Her rise to the top had come via a route not dissimilar to others who had managed to get a foot in the door. After studying for a degree in art and literature, she'd worked briefly at an art gallery. It was here that she began writing for a monthly art magazine, submitting her reviews on openings she had attended. It had been the editor of the magazine with whom she had had a brief affair who'd brought her attention to an opening for a new prestigious art magazine. She'd forwarded her art review clippings and gotten the job. For the past six years she'd been working as a freelancer, giving critical opinions on works of art, galleries and artists. She had a loyal following that respected her opinions; and as such, she played a vital role in an emerging artist's career.

Though the role of cultural gatekeeper had been unwittingly bestowed upon her, she was uncomfortable in it and tried her best to remember that she served the people and doing her job well meant introducing the public to an array of art that would enlighten everyone.

Aside from her work, life for Rebecca had been truly uneventful until she'd met Genevieve. Not that she had anything to complain about — the past thirty years had been good to her, but Rebecca could never have envisioned that she could feel like this about someone. When she'd met Genevieve, it was as if her soul knew the search was over. It was like coming home from a long journey and finally sleeping in your own bed. It was this kind of warmth and security that she always felt with Genevieve and her life had been enriched in a way she never thought possible.

Her most prized piece of art was a portrait Genevieve had given to her. Not only was the painting breathtaking — it was also how Genevieve had first told Rebecca that she loved her. Although Rebecca did not wear a necklace, Genevieve had painted one on Rebecca's neck with the numbers 143 dangling from it. At first she couldn't comprehend the symbolic significance of the numbers, but then with sudden clarity the meaning had become obvious: Each number stood for the number of letters in the words "I love you." Rebecca had had relationships in the past, but they were neither great nor bad. If she had to sum them up, they would come under the term "flat liners"— no ups or downs, no emotional pull either way. It wasn't because she was holding herself back, either. She liked to think of herself as being quite fluid; she just went where her emotions took her. In the last four years though, she'd experienced depths of emotion that she'd previously thought inconceivable.

It was nine a.m. when Rebecca and Genevieve finally strode through the lobby of their apartment block. Acknowledging the chorus of "good mornings" from neighbours, they made their way out of the building. The mild heat of spring lay over the city; the sky was a golden yellow and buds were alive and blossoming, relieving branches and stems of their solitude. The buzzing bees were a welcome signal of the new season now upon them.

The scent of spring, the smell of new beginnings... Rebecca thought to herself.

"I'll see you tonight," she said, letting her hand fall into Genevieve's. They kissed each other on the cheek.

Rebecca's driver was already parked outside in a black polished Mercedes.

"Good morning ladies," Peter said through the open window of the car.

"Yes, it is," they said in unison and laughed. Genevieve brought her eyes up to meet Rebecca's.

"I really love you," she said with such intensity that Rebecca felt a bit unnerved.

"Are you planning on making a confession of some sort, or are you going to do a runner?" Rebecca asked, half-jokingly.

"Neither." Genevieve smiled. "I can't explain why, but it's just important that you know. I'm just being silly. Go on, go, before you're late!"

"I'm going through Westminster, would you like a lift?"

"No, I think I'll walk." And with that, Genevieve was gone.

Reluctantly Rebecca got into the car. Even as

Peter took off, she was unable to shake the disturbing tinge of uneasiness.

* * *

Sometimes life just potters along merrily. Nothing much really happens and weeks go by, with weekends providing a welcome break from the usual routine of having to go to work. At other times, something may happen and a small pebble is thrown into the pool of life. It makes a few ripples that momentarily upset the balance, but then the surface soon calms and normality is restored. And occasionally there comes a time when a large rock is hurled into the pool, creating a tidal wave of havoc and flooding that causes so much damage that the effects are seemingly endless.

CHAPTER 2

Four Years Earlier

THE IVY HOUSE GALLERY in South London was hosting a show in aid of Children South East, a charity which had been set up with the aim of turning troubled teenagers' lives around. Rebecca had been invited to write a review for an artist who was showing her work for the first time, as well as shedding light on the need to help raise funds for such a worthwhile cause. She'd heard good things about the artist through the grapevine, and was interested in meeting her in person as well as seeing her new work.

Guests at the black tie event were met with a champagne reception, including a wide range of canapés created by The Ivy House's award-winning chef. With glass in hand and sipping her champagne slowly, Rebecca moved through the crowd until she spotted the artist. There was no mistaking her — her tall, sculpted body covered by a black, tight-fitting strapless dress served to accentuate the firmness of her body, long hair rested on her bare tanned shoulders, her cheeks were radiant and an enigmatic smile exuded an undeniable confidence. Standing in the middle of a group of people, she looked like royalty holding court. There was humour in her voice while she talked about the graffiti artist, Banksy. Rebecca caught the sound of Genevieve's voice in the midst of saying, "... the problem, and what people can't get their heads around, is that his stance was always anti-establishment and anti-capitalist, but now his work goes for a fortune and he's being exhibited in Knightsbridge."

"But," Rebecca said, moving into the group to stand squarely in front of her, "to be an artist, you have to make art, and to make a living out of that art, you have to sell your work. Isn't it a privilege to make money doing something you truly love, or are artists exempt from needing money? I think there's a distinction between 'selling out' and 'selling.' I don't think you can be accused of selling out unless you change your work to cave in to commercial pressures, or prostitute yourself for the advertising pound — and he's never done that."

There was an instant spark in Genevieve's eyes as they met with Rebecca's. She drank in Rebecca's features — the way her face was framed in long, tousled curls of ebony, which perfectly complemented her subtle olive skin-tone. Her piercing eyes with the teasing hint of grey held a distant, dreamy look and her figure was slender and taut. But it was those lips — those full and sensuous lips — that almost tipped Genevieve over the edge. For what seemed like an age, she forgot to breathe. She didn't know why she was suddenly speechless. The silence continued as the two women stood there frozen in time, looking into each other's eyes. The surrounding group eventually dispersed, muttering polite pleasantries about her work and went to either look at the art or refill their drinks. Genevieve finally found her voice to break the silence.

"And you are...?" she asked, holding out her hand.

"Rebecca." Genevieve took her hand with the intention of shaking it, but just held it — not quite long enough for onlookers to notice that something was happening between the two women, but just long enough for Rebecca to acknowledge that cupid had stung them both with a sweet, sharp and deadly arrow.

Both women strolled close together while Genevieve pointed out her work. Her creations came under the banner of Fine Art Photography, which referred to photographs that were taken to fulfil the creative vision of the artist. Looking at the images Genevieve had captured, Rebecca knew this project was not just another assignment; it came from a place deep within the woman. Some artists provide art for others to enjoy — Genevieve's art was to provide the viewer with an experience that they themselves would never experience. Her photography was about real life. The emotions, which were captured at the very moment the lenses closed, remained, and if you looked at the images for too long you would feel immersed in them. Genevieve was against the recent trend of careful staging and lighting of pictures; her images were discovered instead of ready-made. Rebecca saw in Genevieve a raw and unique talent that she hadn't seen in a very long time.

"There you are darling," a male voice sounded from behind them. He slid his arm around Genevieve's waist and pulled her closer to him so her body slotted neatly into his. He kissed her briefly on the mouth before she managed to disentangle herself from him. Extending her hand out to Rebecca, she made the introductions.

"Paul, Rebecca; Rebecca, Paul." Paul used his free hand to give Rebecca a firm handshake.

"Nice to meet you; I've heard lots about you. It's nice to finally be able to put a face to the name." Turning his attention back to Genevieve, he said, "I'm going to have to steal you for a while, darling. Everyone wants to know the date you're going to make an honest man out of me."

Rebecca felt an instant tightening in her chest and had to force herself to remain calm, put a wide smile on her face and say to Genevieve, "Well, it was an honour to have finally met you and to have seen your work."

"I look forward to seeing what you write about me," Genevieve said with a flirtatious smile that only Rebecca could see, and with that she turned round and followed Paul into the crowd.

Rebecca watched as she walked away so gracefully. She appeared to float through the gathered guests, seemingly unaware of the effect her presence had on those around her as she headed for a waiter and lifted a glass of champagne from the tray.

The night was a great success with over one hundred thousand pounds being raised for the charity and Rebecca had seen more than enough to write an in-depth piece about Genevieve's art and the charity itself. She hadn't had the opportunity to talk with Genevieve again, but there had been eye contact when they were within each other's radar. To their mutual regret, both critic and artist had been swamped with the guests wanting to talk to them.

* * *

Rebecca's car was waiting outside the building. She had chosen not to learn how to drive because she enjoyed her social life and didn't want to get bogged down with all the hassles that go with driving — namely, being breathalysed. Peter, her driver, had the passenger door open — a gesture he knew she hated, but he did it anyway. He'd been assigned as her driver when she had done a two-month stint at <u>Cades</u> art magazine because she worked late most nights.

Peter was sixty-five when he was given a brief handshake and pensioned off as a driver for the magazine. On his last day, he'd informed Rebecca that he was not looking forward to having no work. She had grown to like him over the months and found him a pleasure to be around. He was kind, intelligent, capable, and most importantly, had an easy-going nature. She had offered him a job and Peter had accepted the position for a fixed rate per week, and said he didn't mind working some nights either, which was an added bonus.

He was a widower and appeared to be remarkably unaware of the attraction he held for women, generally spending his evenings in front of the TV. He was a tall, compact, rugged-looking man who had a powerful, resilient look about him. His thick silver hair served to complement his strong facial features, giving him the look of someone ten years younger. His soft hazel eyes could melt the hardest of hearts and in Rebecca's opinion he was just what any "ready-to-date" widow could hope for.

He gave her a little chuckle when he saw the annoyed look on her face this particular night. He played the chauffeur role to a T and quite enjoyed treating her like she was a lady, even though it pissed her off a little. She was the best thing that had happened to him since his wife had passed away several years ago. He knew Rebecca had given him the job through kindness, not pity, and he respected her for that. She treated him as an equal and had never talked down to him or belittled him.

He was just about to close the door after Rebecca had settled in when he saw a woman emerging from the arts building and heading straight for his car. She bent her head inside the car door.

"Can we talk?" she asked softly. Rebecca slid over to the other side of the seat and indicated for her to get in. She felt perplexed by the unexpected appearance of Genevieve and fought to suppress her mixed emotions of desire and fear, feeling relieved when Peter closed the car door and the vehicle's interior was finally shrouded in darkness. Glancing at Peter as he sat in the driver's seat, Genevieve leaned over and whispered in Rebecca's ear, "Shall we go somewhere more private?"

"Take me home, please," Rebecca said to Peter as he put his seatbelt on.

They had driven the short journey back to Rebecca's flat in silence, both aware of the built up tension between them, but not knowing what to say. Peter stopped the car outside her apartment block and this time made no attempt to open the door for her.

They both bade him goodnight and made their way into the building. The middle-aged concierge who looked like a Neanderthal someone had stuffed into a suit looked up from the computer screen with flat, unsmiling eyes.

"Good evening," he said, then promptly returned to reading the football results before he even acknowledged their reply.

The two women made their way up to the tenth floor and for the first time since they had been in the car, the close proximity of the lift forced them to look at each other. Their eyes blazed with the knowledge that they were heading to the point of no return. With the build-up of nerves and tension, both women were relieved when the lift reached Rebecca's floor.

Inside the apartment, Genevieve expressed her appreciation of the flat.

"Drink?" Rebecca asked. Genevieve nodded her head.

"Please." She walked over to the window to look at the London skyline. "Wow, this is a great view to photograph." Rebecca brought the drinks over and handed one to her. They stood there for several minutes, close but not talking, just looking at the view, sipping their drinks now and then. Without looking at her, Rebecca spoke first.

"So, you're engaged?"

"In a way. Look, I'm going to be honest with you," Genevieve replied slowly as she turned to face Rebecca. Her lips spoke in a calm manner, but her stomach was doing somersaults. "I don't know what happened back there; hell I don't even know what's happening now, but I just need to see this through, to see where this will go."

They both knew they were plunging into something far more entangling than a casual liaison, but the words to clarify this remained unspoken. It was several seconds before Rebecca found her voice.

"I forgot to bring the bottle of wine out with me... Make yourself comfortable," she said shakily as she quickly left the room. She stood in the kitchen, her heart pounding. Normally poised and confident, she felt like a teenager on her first date. When her heart had finally resumed something of its normal rhythm, she returned to the front room with the wine and found that Genevieve was no longer there. She put the bottle on the table and went in search of her. Genevieve was in the bedroom, lying in the bed with her clothes strewn on the floor.

Genevieve stretched out her arm.

"Come and keep me warm; I'm cold." She said it so softly it was almost like a physical caress. Rebecca approached the bed slowly, her heart thumping so hard she wondered if Genevieve could hear it. Her magnetism was irresistible, and Rebecca was powerless in the face of it. When Rebecca sat on the edge of the bed, Genevieve moved over towards her, the sheet slipping away from her body, exposing her small firm breasts. She gently stroked Rebecca's cheek with the back her hand, while a small reassuring smile curved about her lips. When she felt Rebecca relax, she leaned over and kissed her gently on the lips. Sensing no resistance, she let her tongue find its way into Rebecca's mouth, kissing her deeply, their tongues dancing sensually together. As she began to unbutton Rebecca's blouse, a faint gasp involuntarily escaped her lips when she realised Rebecca wasn't wearing a bra. Her skin felt firm and silky to the touch.

The effect of being so intimate with Genevieve made Rebecca's head begin to spin. Her body was reacting in a way that was alien to her. She could actually feel the sexual energy exploding from her insides. With her silk blouse now discarded on the floor, Rebecca stood up and removed the rest of her clothing, aware that Genevieve didn't once take her eyes off her, watching her with pure lust. Genevieve lifted back the sheet so Rebecca could get in beside her. At once their bodies fixed together like parts of a puzzle. Rebecca placed her mouth over Genevieve's breast whilst searching for her place of excitement, caressing the inside of her thighs until she exploded with pleasure. Their lips found each other's once again with a slow and intimate kiss, clinging tightly together; it was now Genevieve's turn to find the place that made Rebecca shudder with delight.

Lying in bed, snuggled closely together, Rebecca said laughingly, "Now the pleasantries are over, we can get to know each other."

"Oh, so soon?" Genevieve said, kissing her again and stroking her body, revelling in the sensuous feel of Rebecca's nakedness.

"I do believe there is a certain issue of a male — a fiancé — and you making said person an honest man," Rebecca reminded her. Genevieve flopped back on the puffed-up pillows and took the glass of wine Rebecca offered her.

"It's a long story," she said, her eyes becoming

darker.

"Well, it's Saturday tomorrow and I have no plans, so I've got all night for this story. Are you hungry?" she asked, attempting to get out of bed.

"Yes," Genevieve said, pulling her back down, "but not for food."

CHAPTER 3

Present Day

AN UNEARTHLY CHILL ran through Rebecca's body as she listened to her voicemail. The background noise of music and traffic muted, and movement paused as if time itself did not dare continue its incessant journey. An unrecognisable voice was still talking in her earpiece. Rebecca was having difficulty hearing what was being said. She had only heard the first few words when her world had stopped. Rebecca sat frozen in her seat. She wanted to tear a hole in the world and escape through it. Peter, sensing something was wrong, pulled the car over to the kerb and turned around to see Rebecca looking very pale, the blood drained from her face. Her hand was trembling, gripping the side of the door handle.

Her brain started to function again, reluctantly replaying what she had heard: *Hospital... Genevieve Simmons... accident... next of kin...*

"We need to get to St. Thomas' Hospital now!" Rebecca barked. Peter didn't need any further instructions. He floored the accelerator and swung back into the traffic, racing toward the hospital.

Running through the doors of the hospital's A&E department, tears came to her eyes, magnifying and distorting the scene into a hazy blur. She just about made out where the receptionist's desk was and approached it, trying to maintain some composure. Rebecca was not normally a dramatist, but hospitals gave her a sense of dread. It had been six years since she'd last entered one — when she had faced the trauma of losing both her parents in a car accident. As an only child, she'd had to bear the brunt of her loss alone.

At reception she was told Genevieve had been moved to the Intensive Care Unit and given directions. In different circumstances she would have humorously asked her for a satnav to help her find her way. The hospital was like a maze, corridors led on to more corridors, and all seemed to blend into one another.

Finally she found the ward's blue sign above the door. Intensive Care. They were just harmless words, two innocent words, but they implied so much. The adrenaline was still firing in her body, but her mind had slowed down. Part of her wanted to swing back the doors and rush headlong into the ward, and another just couldn't bear to face what lay ahead. She hesitantly opened the door and stepped into the lobby area. There was another set of doors, which were locked. She looked frantically around her for some way of getting in. Then she noticed the small bell that visitors were meant to press to announce their arrival.

A faint voice greeted her over the intercom. "Hello?"

"I'm here for Genevieve Simmons, Genevieve Simmons," Rebecca nearly screamed.

"One moment please," the anonymous voice replied.

Rebecca's heart was in her stomach; her hands shook and she had to will herself to breathe. The door opened a fraction and a doctor slid through, careful not to expose the ward behind her. The doctor's thinness caught her eye and for a bizarre instant she wondered if she had been helping herself to the pharmaceutical supply.

"I believe a Genevieve Simmons was brought to this ward today," Rebecca said, exasperated.

"Are you related?" the doctor asked. Rebecca shook her head and for the first time, tears started to well up in her eyes.

"No, no I'm not." She looked down towards the floor. Crying in front of people — especially strangers — was not something she normally did.

"I'm sorry, but due to the serious nature of the injuries, I'm not supposed to discuss the patient with anyone but family."

Rebecca could not take in what she had just been told. The doctor wasn't supposed to tell her because she wasn't related? Rebecca looked at her incredulously.

"You're not allowed to discuss her condition with me because I'm not her fucking family? How dare you! How fucking dare you treat me like this, like I'm nothing!" she shouted at the top of her voice.

The sound of the commotion brought a nurse poking her head through the door; she quickly assessed the situation and asked if she should call security.

"She's my partner... you called me!" Rebecca broke down completely. The doctor quickly looked through his notes and then gently took Rebecca by the arm and led her into the waiting room adjacent to the ward. They both sat down on what looked like relatively new chairs. "You are right I am sorry. She had a next of kin card and we have been trying to contact you all day. When we couldn't reach you we managed to track down her parents, they should be arriving shortly."

"I've had my phone off as I've been in a meeting all day, please tell me how she is."

The look on the doctor's face made Rebecca brace herself for the worst. She held her breath.

"I'm afraid she was involved in what looks like a mugging, and as a result has suffered trauma to her head. Genevieve is still alive," the doctor said, responding to Rebecca's stricken face, "but she's in a coma. Although she's still breathing, she's unconscious; she can't respond to any stimuli such as pain or the sound of a voice, or perform any voluntary actions. The brain is still functioning, but at its most basic level."

The walls started to close in on Rebecca.

How can this be happening? Genevieve, who'd responded to her lovemaking this morning, both laughing like school girls in the shower, feeding each other breakfast... And now she was in a coma. *How can that be?*

The doctor was still talking and Rebecca tried her hardest to concentrate.

"There is no single treatment that can cause someone to come out of a coma, however, treatments can prevent further physical and neurological damage."

"I want to see her," Rebecca said, standing up

unsteadily. "Please let me see her." The doctor rose with her and put a hand on her arm, although whether to comfort or steady her, Rebecca didn't know.

"Genevieve has a lot of machines surrounding her at the moment, so it looks scarier than it actually is," the doctor responded, and then paused. "We don't know the extent of the damage so we are just taking precautions. The wires and tubes attached to her are monitoring her organs. If there are other serious or life-threatening injuries to the rest of the body, they'll be dealt with in order of decreasing severity. I'm explaining this to you so you're prepared for when you see her." She gave Rebecca a faint smile.

God, how many times a day does she repeat those lines? Rebecca wondered as she followed the doctor into the ICU. She held her breath as she walked through the ward, trying hard not to look at the dying and seriously ill patients who looked as though their souls had already vacated their bodies, leaving nothing behind but shells. The silence of the ward was interrupted by the sound of the machines, continuous deep, short shunting breaths being pumped into the bodies of the unconscious from the ventilator. And then Rebecca's eyes were drawn to Genevieve, who looked like an Egyptian mummy preserved in time. She lay motionless, as still as silence.

The doctor hadn't lied — there were tubes and wires coming from her blood-encrusted temples, arms and hands. Her face was red and swollen with a large bruise developing on one side. Her hands had so many tubes attached to them they looked like someone had been using them for an atlas, and had stuck pins in to show where they had travelled. Each tube had a label indicating what medication was being fed into her body.

Rebecca stood beside the bed and touched Genevieve's hand; it was surprisingly warm, but felt lifeless. There was no feeling in it, no response. She didn't know what to do with herself, whether to scream, cry, shout, or maybe rip the wires from Genevieve's body and carry her home and will her to wake up and relive the day again — only this time she would not let her go; she would hold her forever.

Did Genevieve see the person who attacked her? What was she thinking at that very moment? Did she think of me? Rebecca felt like she was dying inside. If this had to happen, she wished she could have been there; that she could have held her, stroked her hair the way she liked, held her hands in hers, told her she was there and she would never leave her and that she loved her and everything was going to be alright. Did anyone comfort her or did they just leave her lying on the floor, stunted by their own fear of how easily the path of life changes?

Rebecca heard Genevieve's mother before she saw her. A low whining sound that was barely audible soon turned into a hysterical pitch that clawed at those who heard it, leaving imprints on their hearts; her pain, like a thick fog, choking the room.

Genevieve's parents were being comforted by a nurse as she cajoled them toward the bed where their lifeless daughter lay. As they came nearer the bed, Rebecca could see the grief written in every line on Genevieve's mother's face. She was a short woman, her hair scraped back severely in a tight bun, her slender body shaking.

"Oh God, oh my God," she wailed, tears dripping from her cheeks. Genevieve's father stood beside his wife. It took them a few minutes to acknowledge she was standing there, and the moment they did, the pure dread on their faces was replaced with pure hatred.

CHAPTER 4

Four Years Earlier

REBECCA AND GENEVIEVE spent their first weekend together in bed, watching each other, laughing, talking, taking long, leisurely baths together and revealing secrets only lovers did when they wanted to let each other in, when they wanted to connect. Genevieve had finally relented and explained the history between herself and Paul, but only after he had called her day and night, demanding to know where she was.

Paul was a fellow artist whose passion was painting. If he could exist without sleeping and just paint, he would. It was this passion that had brought them together. She had been attracted to Paul as an artist, not a lover, but she'd been too young to know the difference. She had not really paid much attention to her sexuality, or what gender she was attracted to — to her it was just about a meeting of the minds. Whilst travelling and taking photos, she had slept with a couple of women — nothing heavy — just a pleasurable release. She was not looking for a relationship per se, until she met Paul. What drove their relationship was the enthusiasm, the excitement, the energy, and how they conversed on the ideas generated about the art they were producing. Genevieve had never lied to herself about feeling any great passion toward the man — it was toward what he represented.

Things had moved quickly between them; they were soon live-in lovers and inseparable. More importantly, they appreciated each other's dedication to their given art. It wasn't long before Paul was introduced to her family and he was an instant hit. Her parents were devout Catholics who were pleased she had made a union with someone of the same faith. They knew better than to try and force the issue about marriage with her, but on many occasions Paul would be in secret talks with her parents about making an "honest woman of her," which was good enough for them.

Life had drifted along for the next few years. They had settled into a familiar pattern of painting, galleries, art shows and the like. One day, Genevieve had received an assignment to cover a trial in an African state. She'd grabbed the opportunity and after getting back from Africa, her agent had touted her photographs around and they had been a huge hit. An opportunity had arisen for her to showcase her photographs for a charity she held close to her heart. It was called Children South East and she and Paul had been donating their art to them for years.

It was at a celebratory meal with family and friends before her showcase that Paul had proposed marriage to her in the good, old-fashioned way. He had asked her father for his blessing, he had the diamond ring and he went down on one knee. Sitting there in total shock and looking at her parents' beaming faces, she'd had no choice but to say yes; she had truly been ambushed and there was no way out. So, she had played along and cried real tears, only they weren't tears of joy, but of sadness. It was in this happy, boisterous mood that the party of family and friends had made their way to The Ivy House Gallery.

Genevieve had never been unfaithful to Paul, but she really hadn't been able to help herself this time. Well, she could have helped herself by not following Rebecca outside when she had seen her leaving, or going back to her apartment with her and seducing her before they'd even finished their first drink. But it was done now, and she had to face the music. The fact was that she'd left the gallery without even saying goodbye to her parents or Paul, and she had not left Rebecca's apartment for the entire weekend.

She knew she was going to have to go home that evening, and she knew she was leaving him. She knew in her heart she should have left years ago, but she hadn't, and now she was going to have to deal with the consequences.

"I think it's time I put some clothes on. I'm beginning to feel like a naturist," Genevieve said smiling, but the smile didn't reach her eyes. Rebecca knew Genevieve was starting to erect a barrier between them, but she didn't know why.

"Have you any regrets, Genevieve?" she asked, bracing herself for the answer.

"Yes," she replied, taking her face in her hands. "I regret that I didn't meet you years ago." She kissed Rebecca's forehead, then gathered her clothes together from the floor and made her way to the bathroom.

* * *

The lights were out when she got home. *Is this a ploy to make me think he isn't home?*, she wondered. Now that she was no longer wrapped in the security of Rebecca's presence, the full force of what she had done came at her like a bolt of lightning.

Fuck, fuck, fuck! What the fuck am I doing? she thought furiously. Was she like an uncontrollable teenager, unable to tame her natural instincts? But even as she thought this, she knew that there was more to what had happened with Rebecca than just sex. Had it been sex for the sake of it, she would not be longing to be back with her, looking at her, waking up with her. The physical attraction had been intense and they had needed to satisfy that urge to see if there was anything worthwhile behind it. Both had known there would be, but had they not released the pent-up energy that had occurred from their first meeting, they probably would have exploded.

She opened the front door and walked straight into the dark front room. She saw his silhouette on the sofa from the street lamp outside.

"So you decided to come back," he slurred. He was drunk and holding the empty bottle of whiskey to his chest. Genevieve switched on the light.

"I think it's best we talk when you're sober," she said, mildly annoyed.

"Are you fucking joking?" he raged. "You stay out all weekend like a fucking alley-cat in heat and have the gall to dictate to me when we can talk!" He heaved himself onto his feet and stood towering over her, his face bright red, infused with a mixture of alcohol and anger.

"Look, Paul," she said, refusing to cower to him,

"you're drunk and if you think you are going to get anywhere by behaving in a threatening manner toward me, you have another thing coming. When you are sober, I will discuss with you what we should have discussed a long time ago."

"Oh just fuck off, you fucking dyke. Yes, that's right: DYKE. The whole fucking gallery was talking about you two — the famous dyke art lover and the star-struck artist. Have you any idea how fucking small you made me feel? Not to mention the humiliation of your parents hearing about their fucking pussy-loving dyke of a daughter."

Up until then, Genevieve hadn't been affected by his torrent of abuse. He was hurt so it was understandable, but the bit about her parents startled her. Did her parents really know or was he just saying that to get back at her? He was still ranting, but she was no longer listening — she just had to get out of there. She ran into their bedroom, grabbed her overnight bag from the wardrobe, threw some clothes in it and gathered together her toiletries. He didn't try to stop her from leaving, in fact, he opened the door for her and told her in no uncertain terms to get out.

She decided to book into a hotel for a few days to give her time to think. She wanted to be with Rebecca, but this was her mess and she didn't want to spoil what had been a perfect weekend with her emotional baggage. The hotel room was spacious and plush. A large, flat-screen TV hung on the wall and alcohol waited in crystal decanters on top of a marble dresser. The window overlooked landscaped gardens that would put even Kew Gardens to shame. She was grateful that she'd remained financially independent, otherwise God knows where she would have ended up tonight. She switched off her mobile phone; she didn't want to have to speak to anyone until she had made sense of what had happened in the last few days herself. She didn't feel able to talk to anyone about what had happened either. It was as if friends with whom she could have spoken to about anything on Thursday were not available in this new world of hers. All her friends were straight and had boyfriends or husbands, and no doubt Paul hadn't wasted any time informing them about what a deviant bitch she was.

She called room service and ordered a bottle of chilled Chablis. After it had been delivered, she ran herself a hot bubble bath, filled her glass halfway, and slipped into the warm, soothing water. She sipped her wine and closed her eyes, with every intention of thinking her way out of the mess she had gotten herself into, but instead she thought about Rebecca.

* * *

The following morning she knew something was amiss when she turned on her mobile phone and saw that she had 10 missed calls and a computerised voice informing her that her voicemail was full. The first message was from her mum, sobbing down the phone, asking her if it was true. At that point Genevieve knew that it wasn't just Paul being spiteful; her parents had heard the gossip about she and Rebecca. She sat there with tears rolling down her face. Her parents were the last people on earth she wanted to hurt and listening to the pain in her mother's voice went straight to her heart. Paul had left a message apologising for his behaviour the night before and asking to meet and talk. There were more messages from her mother and one from her father demanding that she "bloody call them and let them know what the hell she was playing at." Her father only used those words when he was seething, and she momentarily felt frightened.

She was twenty-six years old, yet she felt like a defenceless six-year-old and way out of her depth. She wouldn't lie to her parents, so the only question left was would they disown her? Her mother and father were an old-fashioned couple, so she didn't expect them to accept everything, but what she did expect was a little understanding, especially when it came to their own daughter's happiness.

Two days later she still hadn't spoken to her parents, friends, or Rebecca. She had been feeling emotionally drained, but that morning she woke up ready to take on the world. She had made her decision and was going to follow through with it. It was her life and if certain people didn't want to be a part of it, then so be it. She called the hotel reception and ordered a cab. Twenty minutes later she was sitting in her parents' front room, suffering the after-effects of admitting that what Paul had told them was true; that their engagement was off; and she had feelings for another woman.

Her father was pacing the floor like a tiger ready to pounce.

"I did not raise you to be an abomination to God," her father was yelling at the top of his voice as though he was preaching a sermon. Her mother stood still, stunned and grief-stricken. She envisaged all the dreams she'd ever had for Genevieve suddenly smashed beyond repair.

"Please Genevieve," her mum begged, "don't be brainwashed by these people. You're young, beautiful and gifted; they just want to suck the goodness out of you. I know you're a good girl and you wouldn't be behaving like this under normal circumstances. It's this Rebecca whatever her name is; she's messed with your head."

She hadn't been expecting open arms, but this was too much even for her to bear! Four days ago she'd been "Miss Wonderful" and couldn't put a foot wrong, and yet today she was an abomination because she was a lesbian?

"What's this all about?" her father raged at her. "Can you tell me? One minute you're a normal girl getting married and the next we know you're off being a deviant with God-knows-who. Homosexuality is the purest evil of the world, and you need to ask God to forgive your sick spirit! It's disgusting is what it is, and if you don't snap out of this, girly, we'll have no more to do with you. Do you hear me?!"

"Loud and clear," Genevieve said, overwhelmed with sadness. She stood up with her dignity intact and walked out of her parents' house without looking back.

CHAPTER 5

Present Day

LEAVING GENEVIEVE in the ICU with her parents was one of the hardest things Rebecca had ever faced. As much as she was hurting, she couldn't stay in the room with that much animosity. They hadn't exactly asked her to leave, but their body language had said it all and with Rebecca having no legal rights, she thought it better not to push her luck too much in case they banned her from seeing Genevieve at all. As she exited the unit, a man and woman dressed in matching dark suits headed toward her.

"Ms Sheldon?" the man asked.

He was handsome and athletic and he knew it. The only negative she could see was his receding brown hair, which spoiled his otherwise perfect physical attributes. His partner was a slim woman with fair hair and fair skin and strikingly cold blue eyes. They knew who she was because the doctor she'd seen talking to them earlier obviously had pointed her out.

"Yes," Rebecca replied, feeling slightly suspicious.

"I'm DC Simpson and this is my partner DC Smith, from the Metropolitan Police Service. If it wouldn't be too much of an inconvenience, we'd like to talk to you about Ms Simmons."

"Yes, of course," she said, following them to the room where she'd previously had a discussion with the doctor.

Once they were all seated, DC Simpson took out his notepad and pen.

"I'm sorry we have to do this now, but we need to piece together Ms Simmons' movements prior to her attack. I understand you share an apartment with her?"

How very diplomatic, Rebecca thought to herself, but all she said out loud was, "Yes, I do."

"How long have you been living together?" he asked, not taking his eyes off her.

"May I ask what relevance our living arrangements have?" She felt very disoriented and didn't understand what their personal life had to do with Genevieve being attacked.

"I'm sorry if this sounds personal, but it's just procedure," he said, looking a little uncomfortable.

His partner looked intently at Rebecca and interjected, "Ms Sheldon, as you can appreciate, we are starting this case on a blank canvas and we need to know everything we possibly can if we are going to find the perpetrator of this crime. I apologise in advance if the questions are too personal, but I'm sure you can appreciate that we are asking them through necessity, not curiosity." There was no mistaking the authoritative tone. Rebecca didn't know whether this was because DC Smith was passionate about her job or merely didn't like Rebecca questioning her partner, but it made Rebecca feel uncomfortable.

"And I'm sure you can appreciate that my partner is lying in there in a coma and may die for all I know, so I apologise in advance if I'm still distressed and am not responding to your questions like a robot," she fired back at her, the anger and frustration of the day rising up within her.

There was an awkward silence that Rebecca broke with an impatient sigh.

"We've been living together for four years," she said, directing this information at DC Simpson. He duly wrote it down in his notepad.

"Could you go through this morning's events, and if possible fill us in with Ms Simmons' timetable for the day?" Rebecca told him about their morning, although she omitted information about their lovemaking.

"So there was nothing out of the ordinary today?" he asked.

"No."

"And the artist whose exhibit she was attending tonight was a personal friend?" he continued.

"Of Genevieve's, yes. Look, if there's anything else, I'll give you my number to contact me, but I really want to go back and see if there is any change." Rebecca could feel DC Smith glaring at her as if she knew there was more to the story than she was letting on, but she'd be damned if she was going to sit here with this intimidating woman and reveal the intimate details of their betrayal of Paul.

Both officers stood up.

"That will be all for now," DC Simpson said, closing his notebook and slipping it into the side pocket of his jacket. Rebecca stood up, took her card out of her bag and handed it to him, completely ignoring DC Smith. Feeling somewhat remorseful she said, "I'm sorry if I haven't been that helpful, but if anything comes to mind, I will call you. I just don't know where my mind is at the moment." She left the room and its hostile atmosphere.

*   *   *

Genevieve's parents were not at her bedside when Rebecca returned to the ward. The nurse informed her that they'd gone to speak to the doctor. Sitting down beside Genevieve, she took her hand in her own and stroked it gently as tears began to well in her eyes again.

She spoke to her in a whisper.

"If this was a movie, you would wake up now looking like you had just had a makeover and this nightmare would be over. I wouldn't have to sit here wondering if I will be burying you or caring for you." She rested her head on Genevieve's hand. She felt the presence of someone standing by the bed and as she looked up, she immediately recognised him.

It had been four years since she had seen Paul. He still looked the same, but his handsome features looked drawn and his eyes were bloodshot with dark circles beneath them. He stared down at Genevieve, not uttering a word to Rebecca or even acknowledging she was there. He took Genevieve's hand in his and sobbed. Rebecca was at a loss. She didn't know whether to offer him words of comfort to let him know that she understood his pain; after all, he had also loved Genevieve once.

Before she could do anything, she heard Genevieve's mother.

"Paul, oh Paul! Thank God you're here; thank

God!" Paul turned around and embraced her tightly. Her father joined the hug and Rebecca was left sitting there like an outsider.

"What happened to her?" Paul asked as he released her parents from his grip. "What the hell happened?"

"We don't know all the facts yet, Paul," Genevieve's father responded. "All we know is that she was attacked — well, they think it was a mugging — but the police haven't got much to go on. There apparently were no witnesses as far as they know."

"Will she be alright?" Paul asked, turning round to look at Genevieve again.

"The doctor doesn't know; they can't know for sure until she wakes up and they can do tests on her," Genevieve's father said.

"If she wakes up," her mother wailed. Paul once again took her in his arms to comfort her.

"Oh pull yourself together Elsie, for God's sake!" Genevieve's father said, struggling to hold his temper.

"She'll be fine, Elsie, don't worry, she'll be fine," Paul responded sympathetically.

"I hope so, Paul, I hope so," she said, dabbing a tissue at her eyes whilst cowering at her husband's reproach.

"We've just got to have faith in the good Lord; He'll see her through it," her father said with confidence. "It's good to have you back in the fold, son," he said, grabbing Paul's shoulder.

The nurse entered and informed them there were too many visitors and someone would have to leave. For the first time since they had been playing happy family, they all turned and looked at Rebecca. She was determined not to make a scene, so she leant over and kissed Genevieve's forehead, aware that her movements were being watched by the family, but she didn't care. She gave Genevieve's hand a quick squeeze and left.

Peter was waiting for Rebecca in reception at the entrance of the hospital. He sure was a sight for sore eyes and she had never been so relieved to see him. His face was pale, but there was warmth and concern in his eyes and for that she had never been more grateful.

"Come here," he said taking her in his arms. "How bad is it?" he asked after a few seconds.

"Bad," was all she could say through her tears. She had to stop crying. Tears were not going to solve anything and she had to be strong. Not just for herself but for Genevieve as well. Whatever the outcome, she just had to deal with it.

She released herself from the warmth and security of Peter's arms.

"And to top it all off," she continued, "Paul is up there with her parents acting like they are the Brady Bunch."

"Paul?" he asked dubiously. "What's he doing back on the scene?"

"Quite a lot, by the look of it. God, the way they are behaving, it's as if he is their long-lost son and I'm the invisible woman."

"I take it you being there wasn't on their wish-list."

"Peter, they shunned me like I was a leprosy victim. Paul only acknowledged me when they all ejected me out of the ward with their eyes."

Peter was starting to feel angry and resentful. He'd heard of stories like these, where the parents of gay couples lorded it over their partners when emergency situations arose. Instead of respecting their children's wishes, knowing that they would want their partners treated with respect and full involvement with any decisions that were made, they were banished to the sidelines instead. Whether it was a power play or just plain, disgusting ignorance, he didn't care, he just wanted to go up to that ward and tell them exactly what he thought. He was a witness to the great love both women shared. Their love had hurt no one. Standing there in the hospital reception with Rebecca while Genevieve was upstairs made his heart ache.

"Come on, I'll take you home and make you one of my famous toddies." He took Rebecca by the arm and led her to the car park.

* * *

After drinking several of Peter's whiskey concoctions, sleep had come easily to Rebecca. For those few hours that she slept, she dreamt of clear visions of Genevieve, who was conscious and her usual vivacious self. She awoke smiling and was just about to tell Genevieve about the weird dream she'd just had when reality kicked in and the enormity of the situation hit her.

She lay there for a few minutes letting her thoughts run randomly through her mind, then sat up briskly with the intention of getting things in order. She was grateful it was a Saturday — she'd have more time to organise things. It would be better to email work and do a follow-up call on Monday when she had more information to go on. Next on the list was to cancel all of their joint and singular dinner dates and appointments. She knew it was a bit impersonal, but decided to email their friends about what had happened rather than phone everyone. She just didn't have the emotional strength to answer all the questions and knew they would understand and wouldn't be offended. Before all that, she needed a shower and a strong cup of tea, then she would pack an overnight bag for Genevieve. She picked up Genevieve's pyjamas, which she always left folded under her pillow, and put them to her face, breathing in her scent. She willed herself to get out of bed and then literally ran to the shower, knowing if she didn't get off the bed now she would just stay there and wither away.

At six a.m., she took a cab to the hospital, not wanting to wake Peter by phoning him. He'd stayed with her until the early hours, only leaving when he could see that she could no longer keep her eyes open. She made her way to the ICU and was relieved that it was relatively quiet at that time of the morning. She rang the bell and was buzzed in. She was flooded with relief when she saw that Genevieve was by herself. The parents and Paul were nowhere to be seen.

Genevieve looked exactly the same as the day before, but had obviously been bathed. New pyjamas had replaced the standard nightwear the hospital gave their patients. Rebecca smiled as she thought of what Genevieve would say when she woke up and saw what she was wearing. She was not a clothes snob, but there was only so far you could push a girl.

Rebecca kissed her warm cheek and held her hand.

"I'm here," she said to her. "I'm here, baby." She touched her cheek with the back of her hand and watched her, content just to be there, even under such circumstances. She read the doctor's notes on the clipboard at the bottom of the bed and was relieved to see that nothing major had happened during the night and that all vital organs were in working order. Other than that, she couldn't understand the medical jargon regarding the medications they were giving her. She enjoyed the precious few hours she had with her before Genevieve's parents arrived. They were in a more subdued mood, but they still ignored her.

"I brought a bag with items she might need when she wakes up," Rebecca said to Genevieve's mother.

"You shouldn't have bothered," her father spat. "We have everything she needs." Genevieve's mother didn't even look at her.

Rebecca remained silent. *Judging by those pyjamas, you might have what she needs but certainly not what she'd want*, she thought to herself. She decided to not antagonise them by attempting to make conversation. They had made it very clear that they would tolerate her at the bedside for a limited amount of time and that was about it. Even for that crumb, Rebecca was grateful. She was well aware they could stop her visits if they wanted to and she would have no recourse in the matter.

How she could kick herself when she thought back to the many times they both shunned the idea of a civil partnership, never dreaming for one minute that a time like this would come. If Genevieve made it through this nightmare, her first day out of hospital would be spent at the registry office with Rebecca. She would make sure that neither of them would ever have to go through this again.

At midday, Paul arrived at the hospital looking worse than the day before. Rebecca smelt the odour of alcohol as he walked straight past her. Before the nurse had the opportunity to tell them about the number of visitors allowed, Rebecca squeezed Genevieve's hand, said goodbye to her and left. She had never felt so alone.

* * *

For the next week the routine was the same every day, only Rebecca now started going to the hospital at midnight, having been told in confidence by an on-duty nurse that that was the time the family usually left the hospital. She always left when Paul arrived at midday. She couldn't believe how badly he seemed to be taking it. Each time she saw him he looked unkempt and smelt of alcohol. In the midst of her own despair she felt for him.

She knew that he had loved Genevieve and had been heartbroken when she had called off their engagement. Not only did he lose his fiancée, but he also lost his best friend. She had heard through the grapevine on many occasions throughout the years that he was still pining for Genevieve, but for the last year they had heard nothing until the invitation had arrived on that fateful day. Though both women were apprehensive, Genevieve had thought it best that she attend his show, not only for the support he would need but also to try and mend the broken bridge between them. Fate, however, had had other ideas.

When Rebecca walked into her apartment, the answering machine was blipping. She pressed the play button and went to hang her coat up in the cloakroom. She just caught the tail end of the message from her boss, Clifford Stokes.

"...I know that asking you to do this under the current circumstances is insensitive but you are the only person I can trust with such a project. I will understand if you say no, but please think about it. A couple of days in Paris, and if need be, you can be back in London within a few hours by plane." This was followed by messages from friends asking for updates on Genevieve. Rebecca had advised their friends not to go to the hospital and they were all too aware of Genevieve's parents' attitudes toward Rebecca.

Rebecca mulled it over in her mind whether to go to Paris and do the art review. Clifford had been so good to her over the years and he had rarely asked any favours of her.

"It must be important to him if he's asking me under these circumstances," she said to herself thoughtfully as she picked up the phone and dialled his number. She was booked on the seven-fifteen p.m. flight to Paris that same day.

She packed selectively, retrieved her passport from the safe and made her way down to the lobby to wait for Peter to pick her up. She hadn't seen Peter since the first day Genevieve was in hospital. There was no point in him driving her to the hospital every day because Genevieve's parents would not let him see her. They had begrudgingly let Rebecca see her and other than themselves and Paul, they had refused to let anybody else visit.

He held her tightly when she made her way to the car.

"How are you holding up?" he asked, holding her at arm's length.

"Better than I should be," she replied. Peter noticed the dark circles underneath her eyes and the way her veins bulged from beneath her skin because she had lost so much weight. She'd been slim before this trauma, but now she looked like a skeleton. He was convinced that she wasn't eating and made a promise to himself that when she returned from Paris he would take care of her. She had been shutting him and her friends out during a time when she needed them most.

He put her case in the boot and was pleased that she had let herself into the passenger seat rather than the back seat. On the way to the airport he queried her on how Genevieve was progressing. Sensing her unease about the subject, he changed it to her upcoming trip.

* * *

The flight to Paris was uneventful. Even the turbulence, which under normal circumstances would have her reaching for the brandy, had no effect on her. As she entered the arrival area of the Paris airport, she spotted a stocky, well-built chauffeur holding a placard with her name on it.

"Bonjour Madame," he said in a thick Parisian

accent.

"Bonjour," she replied, handing over her luggage. He guided her through the airport to where he had parked the car. As soon as she was alone in her hotel room she called the hospital in London to see if there had been a change in Genevieve's condition. Disheartened, she replaced the receiver; there had been no change. It had been nine days since she had slipped into a coma, but it felt like a lifetime to Rebecca. She unpacked her case and helped herself to the ice-cold champagne, which had been waiting for her arrival in a silver ice bucket — compliments from Clifford — as well as a massive bouquet of flowers. *He's such a sweetheart,* she thought as she inhaled the fragrance from the flowers.

There was a package on the desk with her name written on the front. She opened it to find a ticket for the upcoming show she was to attend and some general information about the artists whose work she would be reviewing. She was sorry that she could not muster up the slightest bit of enthusiasm for the show or the artists. All she could think about was Genevieve. She knew she had to get into her work mode if she was going to do the artists any justice. Not only that, Clifford was relying on her to produce a very high quality piece of work.

After her second glass of champagne, she began to wonder if she had done the right thing going on a trip when she should have been at Genevieve's bedside. By her fourth glass of champagne her emotions and fears had been replaced with a false bravado. Everything was going to turn out okay, so there was no need to worry. She unpacked her laptop, switched it on, waited for the Internet to connect and began her initial background research on the artists.

* * *

The following evening, a fellow British critic named Oscar escorted Rebecca to the show. He was a flamboyant and witty elderly man, and being in his company was just what she needed. He talked non-stop, which was a relief to Rebecca because she was not up for making conversation. He told witty anecdotes, dirty jokes and was very knowledgeable about the art world. Thankfully, the critics only got to spend a few minutes with each of the artists and were then handed a carefully written marketing piece about them, which was fine as far as Rebecca was concerned, as it was their art she was interested in. After seeing each piece, she asked the relevant questions that she needed answers to in order to enable her to write an honest review.

The hours whizzed past and she was more than relieved when the evening was over. She bade Oscar goodnight over his pleas for her to have a nightcap with him and made her way to her room. Her phone light was flashing and she hurriedly dialled the number to listen to her voicemail. There was one message and it was from the hospital. Her heart nearly exploded through her body. The words she would have sold her soul to hear sounded in her earpiece.

Genevieve was awake.

CHAPTER 6

GENEVIEVE SLOWLY opened her eyes and closed them again; the bright lights were too intense. Her body ached and her head throbbed. She was unaware of where she was, but it felt like she was in a void. She tried to touch her head and felt the weight of something attached to her hand being dragged toward her. Within seconds there was frenzied activity surrounding her. She heard high-pitched voices followed by the sound of someone crying. She felt very confused and frightened. She opened her eyes slightly just as a figure appeared in her vision. A tall, thin man with receding hair was standing beside her with a stethoscope around his neck. She looked up into his pale grey eyes trying to work out who he was, and more to the point, where **she** was.

"Glad to have to have you with us," he said in a chirpy voice that in no way matched his sombre appearance. "Do you know where you are?" he asked. She stared at him trying to make sense of what he was saying. When she didn't reply, he continued, "I'm Doctor Phillips and you are in St. Thomas' Hospital." She tried to speak but it came out as a croak. He reached for a glass of water from the table at the end of her bed. "Perhaps this will help," he said, handing her the glass. She took it from him and sipped it slowly. The wetness felt good on her dry throat. She nodded to the doctor and handed him back the glass.

"How did I get here?" she asked, still sounding hoarse. She closed her eyes again, her head pounding. She was trying her hardest not to be overcome by the panic she felt welling up inside. She willed herself to stay calm and take stock of the situation.

"You were involved in an accident," he informed her. "Can I just ask you to open your eyes for a few moments?" She did as she was asked and he shone a thin, small torch into each eye, which sent sharp pains through them. She winced. "Very good," he said as if talking to a child. "Now tell me, do you know what year it is?"

"What year it is?" she repeated, a puzzled face on her features.

"Do you know who the Prime Minister of Britain is?"

"Prime Minister?" she repeated, wondering where this conversation was leading.

"Do you know your name?"

She closed her eyes. She was tired and she wanted this man, doctor or not, to go away.

"Okay," she heard him say as he moved away from the bed. She opened her eyes and saw him talking to a man and a woman who stood closely together. A third man stood with his back to her next to the doctor. She couldn't hear what he was saying, but she assumed they were talking about her because the woman, who would not take her eyes off her, let out an involuntary sob each time the doctor said something, whilst the men nodded their heads. Whatever he was saying to them was not being well received.

"We won't know the severity of her condition

until tests are carried out," the doctor explained to Genevieve's parents and Paul. "People with amnesia frequently forget the accident itself and have patchy memories about the events of the immediate preceding and following days." The doctor walked back to her bedside.

"Okay," he said, smiling at her, "if you feel up to visitors your parents and fiancé are here and I'm sure they are very anxious to talk to you. I will come and speak with you later."

Is this some kind of joke? Genevieve wondered as the people with whom the doctor had been speaking to came to her bedside.

"Doctor!" she said frantically as he began to walk away.

"Yes?" he asked kindly. She felt embarrassed and uncomfortable.

"I don't know these people," she said quietly to him, willing him to understand the severity of the situation and to make the strangers leave.

"It's okay," he said, using his gentle parental tone. "The blow to your head has just left you a bit forgetful. This is your mum and dad," he said, pointing to the middle-aged figures looking at her apprehensively. "And this is your fiancé," he said, pointing to the man with the midnight shadow on his face and who looked like he hadn't slept in a week.

"Look, I don't know these people," she said, becoming more agitated. The woman began rummaging in her handbag until she found what she was looking for and then handed it to Genevieve. It was a photo of the three people standing in front of her, and herself. They were all smiling and looking directly into the camera. The woman started crying and grabbed hold of Genevieve's hand.

"I'm your mum," she gasped, tears streaming down her face. "Oh my little baby, we thought we'd lost you." She took Genevieve's face in both hands and gently kissed her forehead, then moved away to make room for her dad to kiss her. Paul was hovering in the background, looking unsure of himself.

"Go on, son," Genevieve's dad said to him.

He stepped forward and went to kiss Genevieve on the mouth. She turned her head slightly so his kiss landed on her cheek.

"Thank God you're alright," he said, hugging her tightly.

She felt very uncomfortable with this display of emotion and affection from complete strangers.

"How are you feeling?" Paul asked with concern in his eyes.

"Like shit," she said, forcing a smile. The doctor appeared over Paul's shoulder.

"I'm afraid I'm going to have to ask you all to leave now, she seems quite anxious so we have to make sure she gets plenty of rest," he said, smiling at the three of them standing by her bed. They each kissed her goodbye. This time she wasn't as evasive because she was relieved they were going.

Her eyes followed them to the exit and then she turned to the doctor.

"How long have I been here?" she asked as she struggled to a sitting position.

"Nine days."

"I've had nine days' sleep and I still feel like crap," she joked. The doctor smiled.

"Tomorrow we're going to run some tests on you just to make sure that everything is in working order and then we'll go from there. Are you in any pain?"

"Not pain as such; it's just my head that aches," she said.

"Well that's to be expected; you've had quite a blow to your head," he reminded her. "Other than that, how are you feeling generally? Any nausea, stars in your eyes, so to speak?"

"No, just an awful pain down the side of my face," she said, touching it gently. "And a bit woozy, which I expect is from lying down for too long."

"Okay, well there's nothing for you to worry about; you're in safe hands. I'll see you tomorrow." He flashed her a wide smile and went and spoke with the nurses who were sitting around the reception desk.

Lying there by herself, she looked around her at the people whose lives were being propped up by machines. To think that she must have looked like that at one stage sent shivers down her spine. She closed her eyes and went to sleep, only this time her mind was not void — it was full of dreams.

* * *

The next day her parents and Paul visited her briefly, explaining that they were going to see the doctor and they would return soon after. Once seated in his office he informed them of his diagnosis.

"Well, the good news is she's had a CT scan to rule out haemorrhage, skull fractures and other complications, and has had a complete neurological check-up, which have all come back clear. As a result, we believe her amnesia is psychological in nature. There is no effective treatment for psychologically-based amnesias; most of them recover on their own."

"So you're basically saying that we just have to play a 'wait-and-see' game?" Genevieve's father asked, sitting as still as a statue, his back straight as a rod. Everything about him was meticulous and ordered — from his close-cropped grey hair to his polished style of clothing, nothing dared to be out of place. The only thing he couldn't control was his aging — the deep lines around his mouth only added extra harshness to his features.

"Yes. In contrast to the short time it takes to injure the brain, recovery is measured in weeks, months and even years. Recovery is most rapid shortly after the injury and slows down with the passage of time. Many people with severe head injuries end up with almost no noticeable problems and generally do better if just their head is injured without serious injury to other parts of the body, which is the case with your daughter. We must ensure that she has plenty of rest and no stress."

Genevieve's father digested this news slowly; his dark grey eyes the colour of a stormy sea.

"When can we take her home?" he asked.

"We will keep monitoring her for the next few days, and if no problems come to light, she can go home and be treated as an outpatient."

"Well, that's something to thank God for," her mother said, crossing herself in the habitual Catholic way. With a raise of his eyebrows, Eddie silenced her before she said anything else, his eyes narrowing with irritation. Elsie wilted under the impact of his stare, biting her lower lip and sinking her teeth into pink flesh. He stood up, his large frame towering over the desk. The doctor rose at the same time and both men shook hands.

"Thank you," said Eddie. Elsie didn't move until he looked at her and nodded toward the door.

* * *

When Genevieve woke up, she felt aware of someone holding her hand. Too tired to open her eyes, she assumed it was the woman who said she was her mother and squeezed it.

"Wake up sleepy head," she heard an unfamiliar voice say. She opened her eyes and was shocked not to see her mother sitting by her bed but a complete stranger. She snatched her hand away from the strange woman.

"Do I know you?" she asked.

Rebecca looked completely dazed. "Genie, it's me, Rebecca."

"I'm sorry, but I have never seen you before in my life."

"Is this some kind of joke? Because if it is, it's not funny. I have been worried sick about you," Rebecca said in an accusing voice.

"I can assure you that this is no joke, I think I would know if I knew you, and I don't. You've obviously mistaken me for someone else."

It was the look in Genevieve's eyes that told Rebecca she was telling the truth. She really had no recollection of her. A fountain of fear rose steadily in Rebecca's body. Her heart started beating faster; she couldn't comprehend what this meant. She looked for a doctor or nurse, but they all seemed to be busy — and damn! Just at that moment, Genevieve's parents walked in.

"Have you ever met this woman before?" Genevieve asked the woman who was supposedly her mother, pointing at Rebecca. Elsie's eyes swept Eddie's face, unsure of what to say. He responded by pursing his lips and folding his arms defensively.

"No, I can't say I have," she said, taking the cue, the colours deepening in her cheeks. She wasn't lying as such because she hadn't actually "met" Rebecca before; she had only seen her that night at The Ivy House and had not been formally introduced to her.

"She seems to think she knows me, but I've never seen her before."

"Genie," Rebecca pleaded, "we've been living together for the past four years!" Genevieve looked confused.

"I think it's best you leave," her father interjected. "You may well be her flatmate, but we've never met you, and she's too unwell to see anyone. Do you want me to call security?" he asked threateningly.

Rebecca stood up to leave and caught the look of triumph in Paul's eyes, whose previous appearance of an unhealthy pallor had been replaced with clean-shaven cheeks and a healthy glowing face. She took one more look at Genevieve's confused face and started to walk towards the exit.

She was just within earshot when she heard Paul

saying, "Hello darling. I hope I look more appealing now." Rebecca felt as if someone had just brutally stabbed a large knife into the softest part of her back.

* * *

Peter was waiting outside the hospital. Rebecca had called him from the airport and asked him to pick her up as she'd wanted to go straight to the hospital. He was beside himself with excitement when he heard Genevieve was awake.

"Now everything can return to normal," he'd said to himself, smiling. That thought was soon cut short when he saw Rebecca making her way towards the car. He could tell from her body language that things had not gone well. Instead of walking upright as she normally did, her shoulders were cowered over, her head was bent towards the floor, oblivious to the people that were moving quickly out of her way to avoid colliding with her.

He got out of the car as quickly as his body would allow him and walked across the road to where Rebecca stood. She didn't see him and was startled when he put his hand on her arm.

"Rebecca," he said gently. Her eyes were vacant and he felt panic rise within him. "Rebecca, talk to me. What's happened?" He braced himself for the worst. He had seen that look in people's eyes in the army when they had seen something traumatic.

"She doesn't know me," she mumbled, still acting like she was possessed.

"Of course she wants to know you," he said, having misheard what she said. His adrenaline rush subsided. Thinking that they'd possibly had a squabble, he increased his pace to walk beside Rebecca.

"She doesn't know me," she repeated. He was confused. *What does she mean, she doesn't know her?* Then it struck him. She had suffered a head injury and she must have some sort of amnesia.

He grabbed Rebecca's arm just as she was about to walk into oncoming traffic.

"Rebecca," he said sharply, hoping to snap her out of her daze. She looked at him, childlike and vulnerable.

"Rebecca, listen to me, this mess is going to be all right. Do you hear me? It's going to be alright." He didn't know which of them he was trying to convince more.

* * *

Rebecca let herself into her apartment and hung her keys up on the key rack in the passage. *There should be another key there,* she thought to herself. That was how she knew if Genevieve was home or not. When Genevieve worked from home she worked in silence, so the key would be the signal she was home. The flat no longer felt like a home. It was only a home when Genevieve was there, filling the place with love and laughter. Each room held vivid memories for Rebecca. Each room had a story. She desperately wanted to cry, but nothing came. She aimlessly wandered around the flat with her memories as her only companions.

As darkness started to wrap itself around the city, Rebecca sat in her apartment looking through the window, staring blankly at the black water beneath

Westminster Bridge. She couldn't take her eyes off it as the reflection from the lights on the bridge glistened on its glass-like surface. An empty bottle of wine stood on the table beside her, its contents having done nothing to numb her pain. She felt as though she was in one of those crass black-and-white movies where the women were overly emotional or fainted when the stress became too much.

She knew she was strong and she knew she was going to have to snap out of this victim mentality she had allowed herself to wallow in. The candles flickered in the darkness of the room, making objects look larger than they really were. That's what she had allowed to happen. She had let the situation seem bigger than it was. She closed her eyes and let the tension release from her neck and shoulders. She took a deep breath and slowly released it, feeling stronger within herself.

* * *

The next morning she arrived at the hospital early. She was not going to cower in the face of adversity. As she made her way through the hospital corridors, she passed by one of the nurses who had been on duty in the ICU. They both smiled at each other and for one brief moment the nurse hesitated, as if she was going to say something, but then walked on. When Rebecca reached the unit she was informed that Genevieve had been moved to another ward as her injuries were no longer life-threatening. She had a private room, thanks to the health care plan both women had taken out after reading the horror stories in the national newspapers about NHS hospitals.

Once Rebecca found the ward, the nurse showed her the way to Genevieve's room. Rebecca knocked hesitantly on the door, praying that Genevieve's parents were not present — if they were, there was definitely going to be a showdown.

"Come in!" Genevieve called out. As Rebecca walked in, she caught the surprised look on Genevieve's face.

"Hi."

"Come in; I remember you from yesterday."

"Thanks for not yelling for security," Rebecca joked. Genevieve smiled that smile Rebecca remembered so well. It took all the strength she had not to grab hold of her and tell her how she felt.

"That's okay," Genevieve said. "I'm surprised you came back"

"If anything, I'm persistent." She closed the door behind her, glad of the privacy the room afforded them. This room was bright and breezy — a far cry from the overcrowded wards she had seen on her way there. It didn't have that certain hospital smell of disinfectant that normally permeates the air. She sat down on the comfortable armchair that had been placed beside Genevieve's bed. Both women looked at each other. Genevieve still looked quite unwell and the bruising remained prominent on her face.

"One of the nurses told me you haven't left the hospital since I arrived. We must have been good friends — were we flatmates?" she asked.

"Yes, we were, I mean, are," Rebecca replied.

"So I take it from yesterday's performance you didn't get on well with my parents?"

"Well, it's true that I've never formally met them

— they've never come to our flat. As for their opinion of me, well, you'd better ask them that," Rebecca said, still feeling an echo of humiliation.

Sensing her unease, Genevieve changed the subject.

"Would you like something to drink?" Genevieve asked, nodding toward the side table.

Rebecca looked at the array of soft drinks on display and then noticed the framed photos of Genevieve's family and a large picture of Genevieve and Paul in a romantic pose, which must have been taken during their courtship. Shock gave way to disbelief. Were they really trying to pass Paul off as Genevieve's partner? Surely they couldn't be that cruel and blatant that they would use an opportunity like this to try and convince Genevieve she was straight. Rebecca's heart sank. What other explanation could there be?

"Oh yes, the photos," Genevieve said, mistaking Rebecca's interest in them for something else. "They're supposed to help me remember who I am. I've looked at them for hours and I just don't feel any kind of connection," she said sadly.

"Maybe you're trying too hard," Rebecca offered. "Perhaps if you just let your mind think about what it wants to think about rather than force it to remember, something might come back to you naturally."

"I suppose so, but it's just so frustrating. I mean not knowing what sort of a person I was — or should I say, am..."

"Well, you can take it from me that you were — are — a really good person, kind, considerate —"

Genevieve interrupted her.

"Yes, that's all well and good, but they're just attributes. What I mean is — what was my passion? Did I even have a passion? Were my relationships with people good ones? Everything feels so contrived because I can't remember. For all I know, my parents who seem to love me very much could have been a nightmare to get on with, or my fiancé, Paul, could have been a cheating so-and-so and his love and concern for me could just be a big act," she said despondently.

"Well, if it's any consolation, we were very close for four years and I can tell you that you were very passionate about art, and our relationship was a good one." She wondered if she should tell her the truth and just get it over with. Taking a deep breath, she was about to shatter Genevieve's illusion when the door swung open behind her.

Rebecca swung her head round to see Paul walking in holding a large portfolio case in his hand. She was interested to see how he would act without the backup of Genevieve's parents. Would he really act out this sham in front of her? She stared hard at him as he walked over to Genevieve and kissed her on the cheek.

"And how are you today?" he asked.

"Better than yesterday," she replied. Looking at Rebecca, she said, "We were just catching up." He looked nervously at Rebecca now.

"Oh, is that so?" was all he said.

"Yes; it seems that I have a passion for art." He made no effort to disguise the relief that flooded his features.

"Yes, well, I can show you just how passionate you are," he said as he unzipped the portfolio to reveal paintings and pictures that Rebecca had never seen before. Genevieve must have produced them while she was in a relationship with him and she hadn't taken them back when they broke up. They were amazing prints and paintings. The room remained silent while Genevieve took her time looking at her work. She was so engrossed in looking at the images she failed to notice the tension in the room or the dagger stares Rebecca and Paul were parrying.

"Wow!" Genevieve said when she'd finished looking at each piece of her work. "That was intense." She rubbed her eyes, a habit she had when she was tired. "To think I created all that is amazing! Even I'm impressed with them." She zipped the case closed. "Thanks for that Paul; I really appreciate you bringing it."

"It's my pleasure dar —" He stopped abruptly and put the case on the floor. "Is there anything I can get you?"

"No. I don't mean to be rude, but I think I'd just like to sleep for a bit," she said, stifling a yawn. She looked apologetically at Rebecca. "Will you visit again? I'd really like to talk some more."

"Try and stop me," Rebecca replied, smiling, and reluctantly stood up. Paul made no attempt to move and anger coursed through Rebecca's veins. What could she do but leave? She was not about to make a scene by declaring her undying love to Genevieve and informing her that she was not Paul's lover but hers; that he had no right being there; that it was her who should have been by her side coaxing her to remember who she really was. She vowed she would not let him or Genevieve's parents get away with their intended plan. If they wanted to play dirty, she was a more than willing opponent.

As Rebecca was leaving the ward she bumped into Genevieve's parents. She tried to walk past them but Genevieve's father caught her arm. Rebecca jerked away.

"I don't want you coming here anymore," Genevieve's father snarled, keeping his voice low to not draw attention.

"That's not your choice," she replied.

"Don't you think for a minute that we don't know what you're up to. We know **exactly** what you are trying to do!"

"And what's that?" she asked incredulously.

"Trying to turn her into a deviant. God has given her another chance to lead a good and respectful life and I will not let you corrupt her again. Do you hear me?" His words were filled with venom.

Rebecca didn't respond. She knew there was nothing she could ever say to change this man's views so she wasn't going to waste any energy trying, but being banned from seeing Genevieve posed a serious problem. She didn't know whether he had the legal right to stop her from seeing her Genevieve. Genevieve was an adult and Rebecca could prove that they were more than friends — they owned an apartment together; they were named as each other's beneficiaries on their life insurances. Surely that must account for something?

Rebecca's mobile phone started ringing, which

was her cue to leave the ugly scene she was reluctantly embroiled in. She let it ring for a few seconds until she was well away from the ward.

"Hello," she said, grateful to whoever it was that had saved her from spending another second in that man's company.

"Hello darling," Clifford's voice boomed in her ear. "Glad to hear Genevieve is on the mend. I wonder if she would mind me taking you away for a few days? One of the artists you reviewed in Paris is going solo and his agent wants you to cover his first show."

"I don't know, Cliff," she said hesitantly. She hadn't told him that Genevieve had amnesia. She'd had enough of the sympathy that people had been showering on her. She knew it was with good intentions, but it just made her feel weak. She debated in her mind whether or not to accept the assignment. She didn't know how long she could be at loggerheads with Genevieve's parents and Paul and maybe the break would do them all good — it would give Rebecca time to figure out what to do.

"Okay, I'll go," she finally said.

"You are a darling," he responded happily and rung off.

I'm glad someone thinks so, she thought to herself and tried to bury the uneasiness she felt in the pit of her stomach.

CHAPTER 7

FOR THE SECOND TIME that week Rebecca was busy packing for a trip to Paris. She was interrupted by the sound of her intercom buzzing and impatiently walked over to it as she wasn't expecting anyone. She picked up the receiver to be told by the concierge that there was a DC Smith downstairs wishing to see her. Rebecca asked him to send her up.

"Now what?" she muttered. She'd found herself being defensive with everyone lately. Under normal circumstances she got on very well with people, but since Genevieve's accident, she constantly felt irritated and anger was always hovering just under the surface. The doorbell sounded and she went to answer it. DC Smith stood there alone. Both women looked directly at each other, trying to size up the other's mood. After their last meeting, they were both unsure of how they would get on.

"Ms Sheldon, sorry to bother you again," DC Smith began.

"Please, call me Rebecca. Please come in," she said, determined to start their interaction on a pleasant note.

"Thank you." DC Smith glanced around the flat as she walked in, thinking that her own flat would fit just in the living room alone.

"Please sit down," Rebecca offered. "Can I get you something to drink?"

"Tea would be great — if you have the time," she said, nodding her head toward the open suitcase, which was lying on the floor.

"My flight isn't until this evening. I won't be a minute."

DC Smith looked around the room more intensely, admiring the choice of artwork that hung selectively on the walls. There were just enough pictures without the room being overwhelmed by them. Her eyes were drawn to the painting of Rebecca. It was extremely well done. It had captured not only the essence of the woman, but also her soul. Whoever had painted it had a rare gift.

Rebecca walked back in holding a tray with cups on it. Even though she saw DC Smith looking at the painting, she made no comment to her about it.

"So what can I do for you?" Rebecca asked when they were both seated.

"You can start by calling me Isabel," she said, smiling. "Ms Simmons' case has been assigned to me, but I feel that we got off on the wrong foot the last time we met."

"Yes, I'm sorry about that. I'm sure you can understand my behaviour under the circumstances. I'm not normally so temperamental," Rebecca replied.

"Of course, it was only natural. I thought now that Genevieve was awake we could gather some more information from her, but... Unfortunately, due to her amnesia, we are unable to progress any further using her as a witness, which is why I am here." Isabel sipped her tea, then continued, "There were no witnesses to the attack, though people who were in the vicinity did recall hearing loud voices and just assumed it was a couple arguing. As far as you know, is there anyone Ms Simmons was having any kind of trouble with?"

Rebecca didn't say anything for a few seconds, trying to think whom Genevieve could have been arguing with. She was not an argumentative person and it was only on very rare occasions that she ever raised her voice. Rebecca couldn't imagine for one minute Genevieve standing in the street arguing with someone.

"I'm sorry, but no; there's no one I can think of. We have a very select group of friends and I'm sure I would have known if there was any bad blood between Genie and any of them."

Rebecca's radar suddenly blipped. She looked at Isabel and something began to dawn in her mind.

"Do you think Genevieve knew her attacker?" she asked, moving to the edge of her seat. "Is that what this is really about? Am I a suspect?"

"No, of course you're not. We checked out your alibi and it's solid; we just have to cover all avenues, that's all," Isabel said, trying to allay Rebecca's fear.

"So I was a suspect?" she asked.

"Look Rebecca, I will be honest with you. The nature of the crime seems to be a personal one. For example, if it was a random mugging, why weren't any of her personal belongings taken? Secondly, muggers don't generally get into arguments with their victims, especially in broad daylight. That would involve face-to-face contact, which would mean the victim would be able to give a better description of their attacker." Rebecca shook her head in disbelief.

"But it may have just been someone looking for trouble, not necessarily a mugging."

"Yes, that may be the case," Isabel agreed, "but like I said, we are looking at all avenues. I was going over your notes this morning and something struck me as not being quite right. You said she was on her way to a meeting with a prospective gallery owner at London Bridge at ten a.m."

Rebecca nodded in agreement.

"So it seems strange that she would be in another part of London when she should have been at her meeting."

Through all the stress over the past week, this anomaly had not even occurred to Rebecca. How could she have overlooked such a major part of the story? It was obvious to Rebecca that she must have been meeting someone, but whom? Why hadn't she told Rebecca? Now she understood why the police thought the attack was personal. She also was beginning to believe it.

Isabel could see the confusion on Rebecca's face and the realisation that something wasn't quite right.

"Did you check to see if she even had a meeting with the gallery owner?" Rebecca asked, even though she didn't want to hear the answer. She couldn't bear to hear that Genevieve had lied and was keeping secrets from her.

"Yes, we checked and the owner confirmed that their meeting was scheduled for ten that morning, but Genevieve had called him to put the appointment forward an hour." They both looked at each other as if they were thinking the same thing. "Obviously something happened from the time she left you to make her change her plans," Isabel said. She took the last sip of her tea and stood up to leave. "I'm sorry if this has come as a shock to you, but I think it's imperative that we're singing from the same song sheet if we're to get anywhere with this case. If you could let me have a list of friends and acquaintances that have been in contact with Ms Simmons, I would appreciate it."

Rebecca stood up to walk Isabel to the door.

"I'll make a list and drop it off at the station before I catch my flight," Rebecca said, opening the door.

"That would be great if it's no trouble, and thank-you for your cooperation," Isabel responded with a smile, indicating their first meeting was well and truly forgotten. She left Rebecca with mental images of Genevieve and an attacker — someone they probably both knew.

CHAPTER 8

INSTEAD OF RETURNING home by plane, Rebecca decided to travel by Eurostar from Paris to London. She loved the feel of the high-speed train whizzing through countryside with barely time to glimpse the landscape. She sat alone in the first-class compartment, her papers spread across the table as she worked to finish her latest assignment. Her thoughts were frequently turning to Genevieve, hoping there would be a breakthrough on her condition and finding her attacker. She forced herself to concentrate solely on her work and was so engrossed in it, she only realised that they had arrived in London when an announcement was made thanking passengers for their custom. Rebecca hurriedly gathered her bag and other belongings together and headed off the train where she was engulfed by the hordes of fellow passengers streaming their way to the exit. Before she left the station she stopped at a small florist shop on the concourse and bought a large bouquet of white lilies — Genevieve's favourite. She took a taxi from the train station straight to the hospital, determined to put Genevieve's parents in their place.

Rebecca passed through the hospital corridors and entered Genevieve's ward. She went directly to her room and knocked gently on the door. When there was no reply, she slowly pushed open the door to find the room empty. At first glance nothing seemed out of the ordinary. She assumed Genevieve must have gone to the bathroom, but it was as she took in the area surrounding the bed that panic struck. All of her belongings were gone!

Looking at the neatly made bed, she realised it had not been slept in, nor recently been in use. Before she even had time to think, a voice behind her said, "Can I help you?" She spun around to face a nurse she had not seen before.

"Yes," she replied fighting to keep her voice calm and level. "I'm looking for Genevieve Simmons; she was in this room a couple of days ago."

"Ah, yes," the nurse said smiling. "Ms Simmons was discharged into the care of her parents." Rebecca tensed at the word "parents." She was stunned by the news. Her hand tightened around the stems of the flowers, gripping them as if her life depended on it. She had to gulp as she struggled to get her words out.

"When did she leave?"

"Yesterday," the nurse replied cheerfully, oblivious to what that meant for Rebecca. "Her parents and fiancé were over the moon." Rebecca gave a bitter laugh.

"I bet they were."

* * *

Genevieve thought Chester Road was a quiet and moderately expensive-looking cul-de-sac as the car she was travelling in came to a halt outside a neat two-storey house with yellow chrysanthemums close-banked around it as high as the ground floor windows.

"We're home, love," her mum said breezily. All the car's occupants were in high spirits — Paul especially. He had held her hand throughout the long journey from London to Surrey. She didn't feel comfortable with this gesture but felt obliged to let him, as he was her fiancé after all. He smiled at her several times as if to reassure her, but it did nothing to abate the uneasiness she felt about the whole situation. Standing outside the car looking at the house, she willed herself to feel something about it — this was where she had grown up, but nothing felt familiar. Not the large oak tree that stood outside the house, nor the large house itself. Paul and her father, Eddie, collected her suitcase from the car boot whilst Genevieve's mum looped arms with her and literally dragged her along the pathway and up the four steps toward the front door. She felt sorry for this woman who said she was her mother, as she was falling over herself to please her. Genevieve felt slightly guilty that she had absolutely no recollection of her own mother.

Entering the house, a large crystal chandelier illuminated the dark, panelled passage way. The atmosphere felt very masculine. Each of the rooms her mother showed her had the same theme and feeling — large, overbearing furniture, heavy dark curtains. It made her feel claustrophobic. Had her mother not lived there she would have been certain the house was inhabited by a lone male. The one place that did reflect a feminine touch was the kitchen. Light floral curtains adorned the windows and the walls were painted sunlight yellow. The natural coloured floorboards were covered with a colourful Persian rug.

"I think I'll go straight to bed," she said, kissing her mother on her cheek. "I'm feeling exhausted."

"Okay love, I'll show you where everything is." Genevieve followed her mother out of the bright homely kitchen just as Eddie and Paul walked through the door.

"I'm going to have an early night, thanks for everything," she said, not pausing to stop, as though they were strangers. She followed her mother up the dark winding staircase.

"Here we are," her mum said brightly, fussing with the bed sheet and then the curtains before the bellowing voice of Eddie calling her echoed up the stairs and startled her. "Well, I'll leave you to settle in," she said, quickly moving away from the window. "Have a good night's sleep and I'll see you in the morning."

Genevieve waited until she heard the sound of her mother's footsteps reach the bottom of the staircase before she relaxed and flung herself onto the single bed, bouncing upon impact. Looking around the bland, magnolia-coloured room with the sparse wooden furniture, she wondered about the girl who had lived there and what her dreams and inspirations had been. And she felt an ineffable sense of loss and loneliness as she thought of trying to adapt to a world that had suddenly turned itself upside down.

* * *

Rebecca called Peter on his mobile phone and asked him to pick her up from the hospital; he was there within fifteen minutes.

"Where to?" he asked as she climbed into the car.

"Surrey — Genevieve's parents house." She gave him the address from her notebook and he typed it into the satnav. They headed off toward the M3, driving for several miles in silence before Peter finally spoke.

"Have you thought about what you're going to do if she doesn't get her memory back?" he asked, looking straight ahead, not wanting to see her face. He knew she must have thought about it, being the practical person that she was, but he was also aware of how much she loved Genevieve and didn't think she'd be able to let her go. It would have been better had she died than for Rebecca to go through this torture. *At least with death you can get some form of closure*, he thought to himself.

"Yes, I have thought about it, but I can't afford to be thinking too much into the future at the moment... I'm just playing it by ear and seeing where it goes."

Peter let the subject drop. Rebecca turned her attention to the scenery that flowed past the window, admiring the trees stretching tall against the sky. They didn't speak again until they arrived at Genevieve's parent's house.

"Would you like me to come with you for support?" he asked, already undoing his seatbelt. She looked at him gratefully.

"No, it's best I do this by myself." She eased out of the car feeling a false sense of bravado. Her heart was racing, her thoughts scrambled and she didn't know what she was going to say when the door opened, but that didn't stop her legs from marching forward to the house. She walked up the pathway and hesitated for a few seconds before bringing the knocker down onto the door twice. She heard muffled noises in the passage, then the door opened and Paul stood there like a guard dog. Rebecca half expected him to bark.

"I thought we had made ourselves perfectly clear to you," he said in a low, threatening tone.

"Paul, please don't do this," Rebecca pleaded. "What do you think is going to happen when Genie remembers? You can't make me disappear; I'll still love her."

"Not if I can help it," he spat at her. "You talk of love... If you loved her, you would leave her to lead the life she was meant to lead — a decent one, with me. All this fucking love crap..." He was cut off in mid-sentence as Eddie yanked the door fully open and walked straight up to Rebecca, his six-foot-five-inch frame towering over her with fierce fire in his eyes.

"Now you listen to me. You turn round and walk through that gate and don't you ever come back here again!" His face was crimson red and two veins bulged dangerously in his neck. He bent down and whispered viciously in her ear, "Now fuck off while you still have the chance."

Rebecca stood rigid, the menace of his aggression freezing her to the spot. He was like a caged animal just waiting to be unleashed and she did not want to be his victim.

"I believe you've made your point, don't you?" Peter said, walking up the path with a sprightliness more appropriate to a man half his age. He stopped when he reached Rebecca's side. Eddie didn't reply;

he simply stared at them both with hostile eyes.

"This is not the last you'll be seeing of me," Rebecca said looking directly into his eyes, feeling a little more confident with Peter by her side, "threats or no threats." With that they both turned away and walked back to the car. Her hands were shaking and adrenaline coursed through her veins. Peter thought his heart was going to pack in right there and then. Sitting safely in the car again Rebecca's hands curled into two tight fists. Her face turned red as her previous feelings of fear turned to anger.

"Can you believe that animal?" she asked fiercely.

Peter could only sit there in silence, too stunned to speak. Sweat trickled down the inside of his shirt collar. He couldn't believe that a grown man would behave like that to a woman. She was no threat to him — not physically, anyway. Finally finding his voice he said determinedly, "Rebecca, I honestly think it's best you stay away from those people." He turned in his seat to face her, perspiration covering his forehead. "I can't imagine how hard this is for you, but you need to leave it alone." His voice shook, betraying the emotional state he was in. He recognised that these were not people who could be reasoned with and he was genuinely afraid for her.

He turned back to face the front, started the engine, and slowly drew away from the kerb and the house that bore everything he detested about life. The drive home was in total silence, Rebecca was obviously shaken by the incident and Peter knew she needed time to think.

Arriving back in London, Rebecca promised

Peter that she was fine and was going straight to bed. Convinced she was telling the truth, he dropped her off at her apartment block.

Instead of going straight into the bedroom she shared with Genevieve, she detoured into Genevieve's work studio. The room was exactly how she had left it that fateful morning. Feeling drained, Rebecca lay on the sofa she had lain on so many times before — just watching Genevieve work, sometimes into the early hours of the morning. She ached for her and tears pricked the back of her eyes like tiny needles, but none fell. Eventually she slept and dreamed of Genevieve. She awoke with a gasp. Looking through the open blind, Rebecca could see it was early morning. She sat up slowly, trying to shake off the last tendrils of the dream world. She stood up and smoothed her clothes down. After casting one more look around Genevieve's room, she took a deep breath, opened the door and walked through it into a world where the Genevieve she had once known no longer existed.

CHAPTER 9

ELSIE STOOD OVER Genevieve's bed, watching her only daughter sleeping peacefully. She said a prayer to any divinity who might be listening to watch over and guide her daughter to the right path.

If only I'd listened to my parents, I wouldn't have had to go through what I did. She was still angry after all these years about how easily she'd let herself be duped into going down the wrong path. But thankfully, God had now intervened before Genevieve could make the same mistake.

She shuddered as she recalled the first time she'd met Nancy.

It was her first day at university and she had seen her at the fresher's ball. Like Elsie, Nancy stood alone, her small frame dwarfed by bulky clothing and big boots as though the armour would somehow protect her. Sensing that she was as shy and timid as herself, Elsie boldly approached, desperate to make a friend. She'd been at the university for two weeks and while everyone else seemed to have made lots of friends, she hadn't yet made any.

"Manic here, isn't it?" she said, her tone warm and friendly. Nancy nodded and looked down at the floor, refusing to meet her eyes. "What are you studying?" Elsie asked, trying to cajole her into a conversation.

"English literature."

"Me too. Perhaps we can sit together and help each other settle in?" Nancy lifted her head up and looked straight into Elsie's eyes.

"I'd like that."

Nancy was a quiet, unassuming young woman who would shy away from making a fuss or confrontation. She had a strong sense of morality and her caring nature shone from within her. It wasn't long before they had formed a strong bond with one another. The following year they were sharing a room together in the student halls, but then things suddenly began to change.

Previously, Nancy had always wanted to spend time with Elsie, but now she would go out in the evening and not return until the early hours of the morning. Elsie, feeling hurt and lonely, was determined to get to the bottom of why her friend had changed so much. One night she confronted her.

"It's not you, it's me," Nancy kept saying.

"What do you mean it's you? Why is our friendship suffering if it's you that's the problem and not me?"

"You wouldn't understand."

"Well, try me," Elsie had pleaded.

After much persuasion, Nancy told Elsie that she was having difficulty understanding her sexuality. At first Elsie couldn't quite grasp what her friend was trying to tell her.

"Elsie, I think I'm a lesbian!" Nancy finally blurted out. Elsie was stunned.

"What do you mean you **think** you're a lesbian? Either you are or you aren't."

"Okay, then I am," she replied confidently. Elsie looked at her as if she were seeing her for the first time. Gone was the meek, frightened girl she had met a year ago. In her place was a confident young woman who was ready to take the world by storm.

Feeling confused, Elsie held her head in her hands.

"So where have you been going all these nights?" she asked, dreading the answer.

"I've met other women at a bar who are like me," she said excitedly. "Oh Elsie, if only you would meet them — they're so... free, so... gay!" and she laughed at the unintended pun.

Elsie didn't think this situation was anything to be laughing about. In fact, she felt quite disgusted. The very thought of homosexuality went against everything she had ever been taught about the rights and wrongs of the world. She thought she had found a decent friend — but obviously she was wrong.

"You hate me now, don't you?" Nancy asked, her mood soured by Elsie's refusal to look at her. "That's why I didn't want to tell you — I knew you would hate me." Silence echoed through the room. "Well, say something, will you? Say you find me disgusting, say you want to change rooms, just say something."

Elsie had to think very carefully; she knew whatever she said next could be the end of their friendship. All she could manage were a few feeble words.

"I think we should get some sleep and talk about this in the morning." She'd lain in her bed fully clothed and unable to sleep, thinking that Satan had the soul of her friend. She avoided talking to Nancy the next morning by leaving before she woke up. When she returned from class later that evening she found Nancy packing her suitcase. Panic set in when Elsie realised she was going to lose her only friend.

"There's no need for you to leave," she said, trying her hardest not to show the desperation she felt.

"Yes, there is; I think you made your feelings quite clear last night."

"Be fair, Nancy, it did come as quite a shock."

"I know, and I'm sorry for that, but you did insist I tell you."

"I know.... Look, stop packing." Elsie went over and shut the suitcase lid. "I'm sorry," she said, smiling at Nancy. "I really am. Can we start again?"

"You didn't do anything wrong, Elsie. I know that homosexuality doesn't sit well with your religious beliefs; that's why I didn't want to tell you. I don't want to change you — in the same way that I don't want you to change me."

Nancy stood up. "Anyway, I have to go, I'm meeting my friends. I'll see you later." As Nancy got to the door, Elsie had jumped to her feet.

"Can I come?" she asked. Nancy looked puzzled. "If you want to...." she said slowly.

"Great!" Elsie grabbed her coat out of the wardrobe and followed Nancy from the room. If this was the price she had to pay for her friendship, then she would pay it.

When Elsie had met Nancy's friends, she was shocked at how normal they all seemed. They were nothing like the people her parents had portrayed as "disgusting sinners." They were intelligent, humorous and very outspoken about life in general. Each of them was so sure of themselves, so confident, that Elsie could quite understand why Nancy was drawn to them. The revolution of the sixties had spawned a new society that encouraged tolerance for almost everything. Within this group of women, lesbianism was portrayed as an acceptable lifestyle, and those who believed it was a sin were "homophobic hate-mongers."

Although it went against her Christian background, Elsie was soon indoctrinated enough to believe that this kind of lifestyle was acceptable, and that her parents were both ignorant and wrong.

As time went on, Elsie started to develop

feelings for Nancy that went beyond friendship. Rather than thinking about her studies, she began obsessing and examining her friend's body language for signs of affection directed at her. The fleeting glance, the physical proximity, it all counted for something in Elsie's mind. It drew her in completely, and for the very first time in her life she found herself actually falling for someone — a woman. There were rumours going around the university that they were a "couple of lesbos," but Nancy didn't care what others thought; whereas Elsie was horrified. She tried her hardest to ignore the laughter that followed them wherever they went on campus and the rude literature that would slide under their door when they were sleeping. It was always the young men who taunted them; the girls just looked the other way, scared that if they spoke to them they would be labelled the same.

How both women actually felt about each other remained unspoken until the night that Elsie had lain in bed and felt Nancy get in beside her. Without saying a word, she'd planted a kiss on Elsie's lips and had just wrapped her arms around her to hold her closer when the bedroom door opened and a group of students had stood in the doorway mocking them, having caught them at their most vulnerable.

Nancy had jumped up and slammed the door in their faces and then tried to comfort

Elsie, but Elsie had been inconsolable and hadn't wanted Nancy to touch her. Nancy had finally gone back to her own bed and eventually fallen asleep against the backdrop of Elsie's muffled sobs.

When Nancy had woken the next morning, she could barely open her eyes she was so tired. A blurred vision of Elsie came into view and she tried to figure out what Elsie was doing standing on a chair. As she'd opened her eyes wider a scream caught in her throat. Elsie had a dressing gown belt in a loop and was attempting to hang herself from the back of the coat hook.

Nancy had leapt out of bed and grabbed Elsie around the waist. After several seconds of struggling, she'd managed to get Elsie down onto the floor unharmed. Elsie was inconsolable, calling Nancy "the devil" and blaming her for enticing her into a web of deceit.

In the aftermath of her suicide attempt, Elsie had a nervous breakdown. She was taken back to her parents' home where they'd used every opportunity to denounce "the devil" in her. They called her a sinner so many times that in the end she began to believe it herself.

Her young, fragile mind would have accepted any reasoning as to why she had nearly fallen into the trap of homosexuality. She'd tried to make sense of the senseless, but she couldn't — she just wasn't strong enough. She'd finally simply accepted that people needed the "Good Lord" to survive, and now, three decades later, she would make sure her daughter would not go down the same route that she nearly had.

CHAPTER 10

FROM GIBBET HILL, the second highest hill in Surrey, Genevieve stood looking down at the spectacular Devil's Punchbowl, a large hollow of dry, sandy heath. The tranquillity and views the place afforded were just what she needed — a place to think and breathe. She had just wanted to get away from it all: her parents, the doctors, everyone and everything. She felt so alone.

How could this have happened to me? How could my life just disappear? Will it ever come back? She kept asking herself the same questions but the answers always remained the same: nobody knew. She felt like she was living in a freak show, and was actually surprised people weren't prodding her, although family and friends did gather around to gawp at her.

Each day she had to sit there with a false smile, trying so hard to have conversations she didn't feel like having. She wondered how well she had really got on with these people in her previous life. *If they bore me now, what effect must they have had on me before*, she thought wryly.

The only time she felt at ease was when she was with Paul. She enjoyed being with him — they seemed to have a common bond in their love of art and she could well imagine why she had agreed to marry him. He'd been to see her every day since she had moved back to her parents' house. He had taken her to visit their old haunts and never got frustrated by the fact that they were his memories alone and not hers.

She had hoped to try and make sense of the situation, but she was still none the wiser and she still didn't know what to do. Paul had suggested that she get back into her work and had asked her mother to contact her flatmate, Rebecca, and ask her to forward her belongings, but she was still waiting for them to arrive.

Genevieve wondered why she hadn't seen Rebecca again since she had left the hospital. She had enjoyed spending time with her and had been looking forward to seeing her again, but she hadn't returned. She had asked her parents about her but met with such a frosty reception that she hadn't broached the subject again. She did secretly wonder what the cause of such animosity could be — even Paul had been evasive when she'd asked him about her.

In a strange way she had felt more on a level with Rebecca than she had with all the people that came to visit her at her parents' house. Also, Rebecca had seemed genuinely concerned about her welfare. It could have been due to the fact they had been flatmates and she was just being polite, but it had felt more than that — she just couldn't put her finger on it.

She was in such a daydream that she didn't hear the footsteps coming toward her until the figure was standing beside her. She looked up, startled.

"Paul!"

"I hope you don't think I'm stalking you. Your

mum said you had come up here and she wanted me to make sure you were alright."

"I'm fine."

"Do you mind if I rest my weary legs?" he asked.

"Feel free." Paul sat down beside her.

"It's amazing, isn't it?" he said, referring to the enormous, bowl-shaped landscape.

"Yes, it is." They fell silent for a few moments. "Did you read the information board about this place?"

"Yes, but I prefer to think of the mystical explanation rather than the boring one about water erosion." He laughed, continuing, "I take it you've come here to escape the asylum?" She nodded.

"Yes. I feel as though I'll suffocate if one more person tells me what a lovely person I was! Tell me something," she said, turning towards him. "If we were engaged, you would have known me better than anybody, so what was I really like, warts and all?"

He moved closer and put his arm around her, encouraging her to lay her head on his shoulder.

"Warts and all, eh?" he said, smiling. She nodded.

"Well, you were — sorry are — one of the best artists I have ever met in my life. You've seen your work; it speaks for itself. You were also impulsive, and often did things before you really had time to think about them —" She interrupted him.

"Was that an annoying habit of mine? I mean, did it cause arguments between us?" She felt him stiffen. "I take it that's a yes?" she asked, lifting her head from his shoulder to look at him.

"You've got to understand, Gen... When your

work went mainstream, a lot of people became interested in you, and you may have done things on the spur of the moment that weren't the real you — more like your alter-ego, if you like."

"Like what?"

"I don't know, Gen... Just things," he said, looking uncomfortable.

"Paul, did I do something really bad? Did I hurt someone?" she asked, tears welling in her eyes.

"No, of course not," he said reassuringly. "What makes you think that?"

"I don't know, but something just doesn't feel right." She saw a flicker of fear cross his face, but it happened so quickly she thought she might have imagined it.

"Are you remembering something?" he asked, straightening up on the bench.

"Not so much remembering; they're just feelings. I don't know, I can't explain it," she said, feeling frustrated that she couldn't express herself.

"Don't force it, darling," he said, holding her hand. "If you are going to remember, then you will. You know what the doctor said: Just relax." She turned around to look in front of her.

"I'm thinking of visiting a hypnotist to see if that will help me."

"No!" Paul barked and jumped up from the bench, startling Genevieve.

"I'm sorry," he said, desperately trying to sound calmer. "I'm sorry, but I just don't trust those people. They could put anything into your mind. Please Gen, promise me you won't go to one of those quacks." She looked unconvinced but nodded. Paul decided not to push the issue any further.

"Look," he said, sitting back down and holding both her hands in his. "I will be here for you through this. I will help you; you don't need anyone else. We'll get through this together, Gen." He said it with such sincerity, Genevieve couldn't help but feel moved.

"Thank you, Paul," she said, cuddling him. "You're a good man and a good friend."

"I hope I'm more than just a friend," he said, drawing her away from him so he could look into her eyes. "I tell you what," he said, quickly changing the subject. "Why don't you come round to mine tonight? I will cook you an amazing meal and you will be the first to see my new work." He could tell that she was turning the idea over in her mind. "I promise I'll be on my best behaviour — no pressure, just dinner," he said with a boyish grin. She smiled back at him.

"Okay, just dinner."

"That's my girl." He stood up and pulled her up off the bench.

* * *

Paul lived in Surrey, minutes away from Guildford's town centre. They drove along a tree-lined street before stopping in front of a large steel gate. Paul took a remote control from the glove compartment and the gate began to slowly open with a loud creak, revealing a large, mansion-style building. Its architectural design bestowed graciousness on the surrounding houses, its immaculate communal gardens, which rolled on for acres, added to its grace. They pulled up in front of the building and got out, walking the short distance to the very large oak door. Seeing Genevieve's shocked impression, Paul laughed.

"Don't get too excited, I don't own the whole place," he said, pushing the door open into a large formal reception area. "The house was split up into apartments when the landlord couldn't afford the upkeep of it — I'm just over here." He led her across the hall to a white door.

She was just as impressed with Paul's apartment as she was with the exterior. A large, open-plan living space housed the living room and kitchen. The furniture and fittings in both spaces looked like they had literally been dropped out of a designer magazine and had magically fallen into place. It was a contemporary, minimalist dream home. The apartment was painted in white throughout with tasteful art adorning the walls. Genevieve whistled, taking it all in.

"Some place you have here... and tidy." He smiled, leading her to a room adjacent to the hallway. It was in his work studio where she noticed that chaos ensued as he swung open the door for her. Large canvases covered most of the wall space, all of which would be shown at the exhibit later that week. An old, battered brown table that could house at least ten guests stood in the middle of the room covered with paint tins, brushes in jars and old rags stained with paint. It was a manic scene.

"And this," he said proudly, opening his arms to take in all of his paintings, "is the theme of my exhibit: 'Man and his Consciousness,'" he said dramatically.

He explained to her his intention to depict the continual struggle of man and his emotions, "To look behind the veil of man." Paul had visited many people in mental institutions to get a feel of their inner demons and had expressed this in his art.

"I'll leave you to look around while I get supper started," he said, leaving the room. She walked over to the largest painting, which she assumed was the showpiece of the collection. Standing in the forefront of the image was a young man dressed in casual attire. To his left was an image of the same handsome face contorted with rage. The same theme followed throughout the collection — different images of one's state of mind: fear; love; confusion; madness... Paul's art was vividly authentic.

The sweet aroma of Thai food drifted into the studio.

"Wine, darling?" Paul asked, handing her a glass.

"Thank you," she said, taking it from his hand. "Paul, I have got to say these paintings are truly amazing. My God, they're unbelievable!"

"I'm glad you like them, seeing as you were the inspiration behind them."

"Me?" she asked incredulously.

"Yes, you. With every stroke of the paintbrush I felt as though I was caressing you."

He moved closer and softly kissed the nape of her neck. The effect of the alcohol and the softness of his lips sent shivers down her spine. She leaned back into him and let him envelop her with his arms. She felt safe and wanted... and something else.

Something was niggling at the back of her mind, but she couldn't figure out what it was. Was it guilt?

But what could she feel guilty about? Paul was her fiancé. To let someone other than her partner kiss her would have been an act of infidelity, but this wasn't the case. Was it because she didn't really know him? Obviously they must have been intimate before, but she couldn't remember those times. Were her parents and their religious rants perhaps playing on her mind? Surely in the grand scheme of things just kissing wouldn't cast her down into the fiery depths of hell? She quickly disentangled herself on the pretence of wanting to see more of his work.

"I'd better get back to the kitchen before I burn supper, anyway." He blew her a kiss and left the room.

Back on her own, Genevieve gulped her wine to steady her nerves. What was wrong with her? Why was she feeling so nervous, so deceitful? She wondered if there had been more damage done to her brain than just memory loss. She couldn't stand in Paul's studio all night — he would think she was crazy. Perhaps the best policy would be to explain her feelings to him; she owed him that much after all he had done for her.

She made her way to the kitchen. He had set the table beautifully with a white linen tablecloth, candles, and fresh red rose petals sprinkled around, perfectly setting the scene for a romantic meal for two. He refilled her glass and they made small talk while he finished preparing dinner. She was impressed with how he worked in the kitchen. No fuss or drama, he oozed confidence in everything he did.

He laid the plates out on the table and served the

piping hot food. Genevieve took a mouthful of the yellow curry.

"This is delicious," she said, and she meant it. He smiled at her, very pleased with himself.

"I thought my cooking would jolt some memories for you," he said playfully.

"Now be honest with me, did I ever cook?"

"You sure did," he said, bursting out laughing. She joined in his laughter.

"Oh, it was like that, was it?"

"I'm afraid so. On the odd occasion you did something right, like making a boiled egg," he teased.

"Well it's good to know I could do something." Their laughter died down and he looked intently into Genevieve's eyes.

"I really have missed you; this is just like old times." In her tipsy haze she could quite believe him. The atmosphere and his company had worked wonders for her. The episode of guilt she'd had earlier was beginning to wash away.

"I'm so sorry I can't remember," she said sadly, and she meant it. She couldn't imagine what it must be like for him, having a partner who didn't remember him or their life together, and who felt guilty for being intimate with him.

"Don't worry, I have enough memories for the two of us. They'll just have to do for now," he said kindly. She leaned over and kissed his cheek.

"Thank you, Paul." As she went to lean back into her chair he stopped her and took her face in his hands, then gently, almost paternally, kissed her softly on the lips. She liked the sensation of feeling his soft lips on hers. She kept her eyes open, watching him angle his head to kiss her more deeply. When she didn't move back he put a little more pressure into the kiss. Her mouth was dry with anticipation and fear.

She could feel his stubble rubbing the top of her lip and she immediately winced, fighting the temptation to pull away from him. He used his tongue to part her lips and at that stage something jolted in her. She immediately withdrew. Something was definitely up. Something just wasn't right. There was something about him that was bothering her. Whether it was to do with him physically or emotionally she didn't know.

"I'm sorry," she said, standing up.

"No, I'm sorry. I shouldn't have done that. Please, sit down and finish your meal," he pleaded.

"I will; I just need to freshen up a little."

"Gen, I really am sorry if I've made you feel uncomfortable."

"It's not you, Paul, it's me."

"There's nothing wrong with you Gen; you're just pushing yourself too hard." She smiled.

"I take it that is another one of my traits?"

"Yes, but it's what makes you such a great artist," he said sincerely. She was grateful for the diplomatic way he handled the situation.

She excused herself and went to the bathroom. Splashing cold water on her face she tried to calm her beating heart. She looked at herself in the mirror.

"Are you a virgin?" she asked herself. "Is that what all this is about?" She shook her head. "Now I'm going crazy, talking to myself," she said. "I must be crazy!" she concluded. "There's a drop-dead gorgeous guy less than fifty feet away; intelligent;

fantastically talented; great cook; caring and understanding; and obviously in love with me even though I'm being neurotic and standing in his bathroom like a sodding nun! God, if this is me I'm glad I don't remember anything about myself!"

She was interrupted by a soft tap on the bathroom door.

"Gen? Is everything alright?" Paul asked.

"Yes, I'll be out in a second," she called. She ran her fingers through her hair, told herself off in the mirror and went back to the kitchen. They ate the rest of their supper, stopping at intervals to talk about Paul's upcoming show. It had been rescheduled the day Genevieve was attacked.

"Are you nervous?" she asked, eating the last mouthful of food on her plate.

"Yes and no," Paul said, as he went to the wine rack to get another bottle. "Yes, because some of the fiercest critics will be there, and no, because you'll be by my side. Top-up?" he asked, the bottle of wine hovering over her glass.

"Yes, please," she said.

"Why don't we go into the lounge and make ourselves comfortable? I'll clear up later."

Several photo albums were scattered on the coffee table. Once they were seated side by side, Paul brought an album onto his lap. They were filled with photos of Paul and Genevieve. Even though she couldn't remember anything about the pictures, she could see that that they were happy as a couple. He also showed her DVDs of holidays they had been on together and various family gatherings. When Paul finally kissed her again later in the evening, she made an effort not to resist.

CHAPTER 11

"COME ON, IT'S BEEN well over a month and you've been living like a hermit," Rebecca's friend, Tia, bellowed down the telephone.

"No," Rebecca answered, "I have not been in hiding; I have been working my arse off —"

Tia interrupted her, "All the more reason to come out and let your hair down. Come on, two drinks and you can return to your castle," she said playfully. Rebecca reminded herself that she hadn't seen her friend in weeks and she could do with some company other than her work colleagues.

"Okay," she said with a smile in her voice.

They arranged to meet in a bar in Soho later that evening. She spent the rest of the afternoon catching up on household chores and cleaning Genevieve's work studio. She'd received a request from Genevieve's mother to forward her belongings, and rather than cause a scene, she'd just packed some of Genevieve's clothes, her camera and one of her paintings, all of which was now in the hallway awaiting collection. The past month had been hard, having had no contact with Genevieve at all, but Rebecca had thrown herself into her work, often returning home well after midnight only to be out reviewing or writing early the next morning. She had even broken her number one rule of not working on weekends. No one knew how hard it was when, no matter how or with whom she surrounded herself, there always came a point when she had to turn off the lights and finally go to bed — alone.

Several hours later, Rebecca had a quick shower, dressed casually, applied a small amount of makeup and left her apartment. She arrived at the bar first. Tia was working nearby so she wouldn't have to wait that long. She ordered a glass of white wine and sat down at one of the vacant tables. Looking at the Friday night crowd made her think of how different the gay scene was since she had very briefly passed through it many years ago. The bars were now more stylish, the women younger, more feminine, and more confident of their sexuality. A lot had changed in the space of only a few years.

She was sipping her wine when she felt someone brush against her. She looked up and for a second had to do a double-take. Dressed in soft pastel colours, the woman standing before her looked nothing like the police officer who had once made her feel like she was being interrogated. She appeared softer and more approachable.

"Isabel," Rebecca said, smiling.

"Rebecca," Isabel said, returning the smile. Both women were quiet. Rebecca, because she was shocked to see Isabel in a gay bar, and Isabel, because she felt exposed in front of this woman who sat there as much in control as she always was.

"How are things?" Isabel asked, having finally found her voice.

"As well as they could be under the circumstances," Rebecca said. Isabel saw the pain in Rebecca's eyes.

"Do you mind if I join you?" she asked.

"Are you here alone?" Rebecca asked.

"No, there're a few of us here; but they won't miss me. I'll just get my drink." Within a few minutes, Isabel was seated at the table with Rebecca. "I'm sorry about how things have turned out for you, Rebecca," she said sympathetically. "I've met Genevieve a few times and she seems a very nice person." Rebecca hated that this stranger had seen Genevieve more times than she had. "This whole situation must be very frustrating for you," Isabel added.

"Yes, you could say that. Are you any closer to finding out who was responsible for attacking her?"

"I'm afraid not." Isabel sighed. "I interviewed all of the people you gave me on the list and they all have air-tight alibis, and to be honest with you, none of them seemed to have a motive for such a vicious attack."

"How is she?" Rebecca asked, not wanting to, but needing to know.

"Well, she looks fine to me, but then again I don't know her in a personal capacity."

"So this is what you do in your spare time when you're not looking for muggers or murderers — hang out in gay bars?" Rebecca asked, changing the subject. Isabel was unsure whether she was being genuine or slighting her.

"We all get some time off for good behaviour, believe it or not, and what better place to spend my free time than with women of my own kind." There, she had said it. No more confusion, no more "Is she or isn't she?" She had told her outright that she was a lesbian. She didn't expect a reaction, and she never got one. Right at that moment, Tia joined them and embraced Rebecca as she rose from her chair.

Watching Rebecca hold Tia in her arms, Isabel couldn't help but think again how beautiful Rebecca was. She had thought so the first day she had met her in the ICU. She had been unnerved that day, but the second time she saw her at her apartment she felt more at ease. She didn't know if she was intruding now that her friend had arrived, but thought she'd better find out.

"I'll let you enjoy the rest of your evening then," she said, getting up.

"Please don't leave on my account," Tia said. "I'm Tia, nice to meet you. I'll get some more drinks in; wine is it?" she asked. Isabel nodded.

"She would make a good detective," Isabel joked as Tia went to the bar. She was surprised when Rebecca laughed so easily; it was unexpected. Her features softened, revealing a more vulnerable side to her. She was glad of the distraction when Tia brought the drinks back over to the table.

"So," Tia began when she had sat down, "how do you know each other, then?" Isabel looked uncomfortable so Rebecca replied, "Isabel is the detective investigating Genie's attack."

"Oh," Tia said. "Don't I feel like I've put my number tens in it?" The three women sat quietly for a few awkward moments. Looking at Rebecca and Tia, Isabel saw a glimpse of the damage that had been done to the two women who'd literally had their loved one torn from their lives. Tia broke the spell.

"I take it there's still no news then?" she asked Isabel directly.

"No, I'm afraid there's not."

"This really makes me fucking mad," Tia said angrily. "Some bastard has attacked someone in broad daylight, ruined God knows how many lives, and is walking about out there scot free. Where's the justice in that, can you tell me?" she asked, gulping a mouthful of wine.

"We will catch who did this to her one day," Isabel responded. "Either through Ms Simmons' memory recovery or something we might have overlooked because we didn't think it significant at the time. This person is bound to talk to someone about it."

Isabel felt taken aback by Tia's criticism, which she felt was aimed at her capability of handling the case. She could understand her frustration, but she'd been doing the best she could.

"How's Genevieve's rehabilitation progressing?" Rebecca asked, tactfully changing the subject. She didn't like the path the conversation was going. As much as she agreed with Tia's feelings, they weren't going to get anywhere taking it out on Isabel. After all, she was one of the good guys in this mess.

"From what Mrs Simmons tells me she's doing very well, but —" she stopped before she said another word and began toying with her glass of wine.

"But what?" Rebecca asked, leaning towards her, the fragrance of her perfume making Isabel feel heady.

"Look, I shouldn't even be discussing this case with you," Isabel said, leaning away from Rebecca. She took a few moments to weigh up the options. What she was about to tell her had no direct bearing on the case so it really shouldn't be a problem.

"We are under direct orders not to mention you or any of her friends who are gay. Basically, we're working in the dark with our hands tied behind our backs. As far as Ms Simmons is concerned, the only people who have been in her life are her parents, fiancé and childhood friends."

Tia looked dumbfounded and tears welled up in her eyes. The loss of her friend and the heartache it was causing Rebecca sent a crippling torrent of sadness through her.

"I'm sorry if you find it upsetting," Isabel said, her eyes on Tia.

"But is this legal — what her parents are doing? I mean, how can they lie to Genie and get away with it? Why can't you tell her the truth?" Tia asked incredulously.

"They aren't doing anything illegal. If I had my way I would tell her, but the family has made it clear to my superiors that any kind of information we give her that could cause a setback to her rehabilitation would result in action being taken against them. They only have Rebecca's word that there even was a relationship. Genevieve's whole family is denying it, saying they were only flatmates, so there is nothing we can do until she remembers something," Isabel said, looking and sounding frustrated.

"So I'm just stuck in this situation with no way out," Rebecca said dejectedly.

"Look, let me take you both out to dinner. I know this great Italian restaurant around the corner," Isabel said, trying to repair some of the damage she felt she had done.

"I love Italian food," Tia said, brightening up immediately. "What we waiting for?"

That's Tia for you, Rebecca thought, smiling. *Her emotions change direction like the wind.*

After the shaky start to the evening, things improved rapidly. Rebecca and Tia were impressed with Isabel's choice of restaurant and like three single teenage girls, they went bar crawling. By midnight, the three women were exhausted, but totally exhilarated, and the alcohol was only partly the cause. Tia declined the invitation for a nightcap at Rebecca's place because her parents were staying with her for the weekend, but Isabel accepted and they caught a taxi home.

Inside Rebecca's apartment, both women sat on a sofa opposite each other. Music played softly in the background and a bottle of cold champagne relaxed in the ice bucket in the middle of the coffee table. Neither woman could remember the last time they had been so drunk.

"I'm dreading to think what price we're going to pay for this tomorrow," Rebecca said, taking another sip of champagne. Isabel nodded in agreement.

"But that's the beauty of living in the now; you enjoy every present moment to the fullest," she said, raising her glass to Rebecca.

"And sod the consequences," Rebecca said, raising her glass to Isabel.

"Yes, as long as it's within the law," Isabel joked. "Did Genevieve paint your portrait?" she asked her more seriously whilst pointing at the image hung on the wall. Rebecca closed her eyes.

"Yes," she said softly.

"It's amazing. Do you ever think she'll find her way back to you?"

"I honestly don't know, Isabel. A part of me thinks she will, because I believe she inherently knows who she is and it doesn't matter how many times they ram lies down her throat about who they want her to be, her true self will eventually out itself."

"I wonder if any of them realise, ever, the disasters they are creating. I mean these families that force lies upon their children — that homosexuality is a lifestyle choice that can be changed with a click of their fingers...."

"So you believe being gay is biological as opposed to the environment argument?" Rebecca asked, playing devil's advocate. Isabel shrugged.

"Let's look at it like this. When I was growing up I knew I didn't like boys in the same way other girls knew they did. Why anyone would believe that people would choose to join a group that people despise so much that they turn families against each other is beyond me. It's not like joining a millionaire's club where everyone looks up to you, where you're held in great regard and people want to be like you. The club we're in you're more likely to be attacked than admired!" She drank some more champagne, enjoying the cool sensation in her throat.

"To be honest with you," Isabel continued, "whenever I've heard or read of people discussing homosexuality, it's as if they're discussing an insect, something totally different than a human being. It's like asking if it's natural for men to find blondes attractive. And then there's the terminology — the opposite of 'natural' is 'unnatural,' but how can

something nature creates be unnatural? Not to
mention the lame arguments that homosexuality
involves using body parts in ways that nature clearly
didn't intend. So what about kissing? The mouth and
lips were not designed for it, or — shock, horror —
nor were they designed for oral sex. People will try to
use any kind of propaganda to justify their belief
system," Isabel said, becoming more animated.

"I know what you mean. Listen to this," Rebecca
said as she picked up a newspaper from the coffee
table and found the page she wanted. She began to
read the first paragraph aloud, "A lesbian novel was
banned after official medical advice said it would
encourage female homosexuality and lead to a social
and national disaster. In nineteen twenty-eight,
Radclyffe Hall's <u>The Well Of Loneliness</u>, which got
no more racy than 'she kissed her full on the lips like
a lover,' led to an obscenity trial, which considered
the implications of the national shortage of men and
two women in bed making beasts of themselves...."
Rebecca laughed sarcastically.

"I mean, can you just imagine the social
brainwashing that went on in nineteen twenty-eight
when most women didn't have the opportunity to hear
unbiased information?" she continued. "They were
indoctrinated with male propaganda, and still are
today. How many women do you see making the
news — and I mean making it — from their own
perspectives? Not bloody many I'll tell you."

Isabel nodded and carried on Rebecca's line of
thought.

"I think there's a problem with all sorts of
information. You don't know how many times I've

had conversations with people and they all talk about the same subjects: whatever's in the media. I'd be hard pushed to find someone with a view that differs from the paper's stance. I can tell exactly who reads what just by listening to what they say."

Rebecca shook her head sadly, adding, "Do you know, I heard that when Labour got into power the reason why they wanted so many women in the House of Commons was because it was easier to get unpopular bills pushed through. Now that may sound like a conspiracy theory, but there are actual figures that showed that women voted a lot more for the government bills than men did."

"So what we have concluded here this evening is that people just find it near impossible to think for themselves or — God forbid — out of the box!" said Isabel with an attempt at a grave expression on her animated features.

"Yes," Rebecca said, "because if you think out the box you are instantly demonised and so deemed unnatural. It's like that analogy about the nails in the fence — which is the first one to get whacked?"

"The one that stands out," they said in unison and laughed.

"I think that calls for another bottle of champagne; what do you think?" Rebecca asked.

"Sounds good to me."

Rebecca walked into the kitchen to get another bottle while Isabel relaxed back into the sofa. She had really enjoyed the evening and found Rebecca more interesting than she'd originally thought. She wasn't going to kid herself — she knew she had feelings for her and that they went further than the friendship

Rebecca was offering. She had never been in this situation before; it was normally her that was being chased, not the other way round. *I have to play this one carefully*, she thought to herself. She didn't want to overstep the mark and lose her as a friend, but she didn't know if she could handle being so close to her and having to hide her feelings at the same time.

Rebecca made her way back from the kitchen to the living room. As she opened the champagne and bent over to pour the liquid into the glass, Rebecca was so close, Isabel was tempted to kiss her.

"Do your colleagues know about your sexuality?" Rebecca asked.

"Some do; it's not something I go around yelling at the top of my lungs. I tend to tell people on a need-to-know basis; i.e. a guy asks me out and I tell him no, because I don't date guys. What they choose to do with that information is up to them. Can I ask you something, off the record?" Isabel said curiously.

"Now is as good a time as any," Rebecca responded, refilling her own glass.

"The situation with Paul – I don't quite get the connection," she said, knowing she had to tread carefully.

"Ah Paul... Poor, bloody Paul. Would you like the abridged version or the unabridged version?"

"Well, seeing as I've got a great deal of time, the unabridged." It was obvious from Rebecca's facial expression that this period was still difficult to talk about. She took a long sip of her champagne.

"Paul and Genie were dating for a few years before we met," she said with a sigh. "In fact, he had proposed to her the very same day we met. It was a kind of instantaneous attraction for us. Don't get me wrong, we never made any excuses for what we did — it was a despicable thing to do to someone and we have no one to blame but ourselves for our behaviour — but we couldn't help ourselves. Well, that's a lie; we could have prevented it from happening, but we chose not to and as a result a lot of people got hurt — especially Paul. He went through a lot. He was angry at her deception and the humiliation of her leaving him for another woman; angry that the trust he thought the foundation of their relationship was built on turned out to be a pack of lies." Rebecca took another sip and then continued.

"Things got nasty, people took sides — mostly Paul's, especially all of her family and friends — and when she finally peeled off the mask about her sexuality and told them she was staying with me, she just stopped hearing from any of them altogether. If she called, they either wouldn't take her call or they'd say they would call her back but never did. She finally got the message and stopped calling them as well. And then out of the blue Paul's invitation turns up..."

"...on the day that Genevieve was attacked," Isabel finished for her.

CHAPTER 12

SO FAR, APART FROM a couple of hitches at the beginning, Paul's plan was working out perfectly, he happily reported to Genevieve's parents. He couldn't help but feel happy and optimistic about how the last few weeks had panned out. Due to fate, Genevieve was back in his life and so long as she couldn't remember her past in the near future, she would remain there.

He had been very careful and skilful at enveloping Genevieve in a bubble of security. With her parents backing him, it was only a matter of time before she had the wedding ring on her finger, and regardless if she finally remembered Rebecca, it would be too late. The deed would have been done.

"She does seem more content these days," Elsie said, putting two cups of tea on the table for Eddie and Paul.

"So, what's the next step then?" Eddie asked Paul, completely ignoring what Elsie had said.

"Well, I think it's best if I broach the subject of marriage again. It will give her a sense of security," Paul said, sipping his tea.

"Yes, I think you're right. Has she mentioned that woman again?" Eddie asked, not even attempting to hide his disdain.

"No, not a word. There's no reason for her to either; I try to keep her mind in the present as much as possible. We don't talk about her life in London."

"I'd hardly call it a life," Eddie said. The

doorbell rang and Eddie went to see who it was. Paul heard his name being called from the hallway.

"Can you give me a hand?" Eddie asked, nodding toward the delivery driver who was unloading boxes. "It's Genevieve's stuff."

"I'd be more than happy to," Paul said, trying to conceal his elation.

Long after his break-up with Genevieve, when the humiliation had given way to anger, Paul knew the time would come when he'd get his own back on Rebecca. He had made no threats, no demands, no begging phones calls. He had left them to get on with their seedy lives and had internalised his rage. He drank whiskey like there was no tomorrow, he slept with countless faceless women and discarded them the next day as if they were merely rubbish. He painted dark, violent images until his arms ached and he could no longer hold a paintbrush.

If it wasn't for the intensity of his rage he would have curled up and died. He never knew that the human mind could hurt so much; that somebody could inflict a pain that felt like a knife being plunged into you again and again as the endless images of Genevieve and Rebecca ravaged his already tormented mind. Then Genevieve's star just got brighter. Her art reviews were now in the popular media, no doubt pushed there by her association with Rebecca. She was no longer in contact with her parents or any of their mutual friends, so it was hard to find out what was happening in her personal life, whether she was happy or not.

It was Genevieve's parents who had lit the path for him to find his way back.

After not returning their calls for several months he had bumped into Elsie by accident. It was early in the day and he was drunk. She persuaded him to go home with her so they could talk. Several hours later, after a hot bowl of homemade chicken soup and lots of water, the three wounded souls sat together and grieved over the loss of Genevieve. For the first time since it had happened, he cried until his body shook uncontrollably. For hours, Elsie held him in her arms and comforted him the best she could.

"You've got to understand, Paul, Genevieve is blinded by an illusion. It's not real, what she thinks she feels. A hotshot critic showed her a little attention and she got carried away with the emotion of it all. Now that she's amongst those kinds of people, she thinks their behaviour is acceptable," Elsie explained.

"Elsie is right, Paul," Eddie added. "It's that group mentality thing where because a group of people is doing it, you think you may as well do it too. She was most probably frightened of settling down just yet. Paul, I know my daughter and I'm telling you now: There is no way on this earth that girl is a homosexual — it's just not possible. Homosexuality is an abomination to the natural human reproductive process. Humans are not supposed to be attracted to the same sex. Our bodies were designed perfectly for one male and one female."

"Why is she still with her then?" Paul asked with a childish whine.

"Because she's not well, Paul," Elsie said gently. "And it doesn't help that she's dazzled by the lifestyle of these people. Remember the saying, The road to Hell is paved with gold? Well, I thought we had taught her better than to be materialistic, but she's always been an impulsive girl, you know that."

"It's a wicked disease, this homosexuality. The victims of it believe there isn't a cure for it — if only they would just trust in the Lord to show them the light. That's where the problem lies: No faith," Eddie said, shaking his head. "And the victims are brainwashed into thinking that it is completely natural and that it's okay, but it's not okay," he said angrily, "especially when it's my daughter!" He thumped his hand down on the table, sending a shudder that caused the cups to lift off their saucers.

"You spent a lot of time with her. Did she ever show any kind of inclination of that sort before?" Elsie asked, trying to diffuse her husband's anger.

"No, never." Paul shook his head. "We were happy — or so I thought. She had never complained."

Emotionally drained, Paul had spent the night in Genevieve's old bedroom. In bed, he pressed his nose against the pillow, inhaling deeply to see if he could get a scent of her,

such was his desperation. The next morning
he woke up knowing it was time to move on.
He was determined to drive out the demons
that dwelled within. He quit drinking, and
with a plan of action in his mind, he no longer
felt as if he were drowning. He had finally,
slowly, begun to swim.

CHAPTER 13

EDDIE SAT TRANSFIXED in his chair with teeth clenched tight, his hand gripping a glass of whiskey so hard his knuckles were white. Though he appeared quite still on the outside, inside he was like a raging volcano. He could not believe this was happening to his family. This disastrous situation had changed all of their lives forever. He recalled memories of Genevieve growing up — she had wanted to follow him everywhere and he loved nothing more than turning around and finding her there, looking up at him with those eyes that could melt anybody's heart. He knew he would lose her one day, as every father does when a daughter flies the family nest and settles down to make her own family, but he had certainly never envisioned it would be to a woman.

When Genevieve had brought Paul home, Eddie had been taken with him immediately. He was a good Christian young man, had respect for him and Elsie, and was a hard worker. He was bitterly disappointed and disgusted with Genevieve when he found out she had left Paul for Rebecca. That she had chosen to turn her back on her family and their values for a woman she had only just met was beyond his comprehension.

"Do you think this is plan of ours is going to work?" Elsie asked from across the room.

"Of course it will work," Eddie snapped. "We

have complete control over her. How can it not work?"

"But what if she remembers?" Elsie asked meekly.

"She won't," Eddie scoffed. "She is going to marry Paul and that will be the end to all of this nonsense. Look at how happy she is! If she was that way inclined, do you really think she would be seeing Paul again? Facts speak for themselves."

"She will make a lovely bride," Elsie beamed.

"Yes, she will," he said, his anger momentarily subsiding to share in her fantasy. "Paul knows what he's doing."

"What are we going to do about... the problem?" Knowing that she couldn't bring herself to say Rebecca's name, Eddie answered as if she had said it.

"It will go away eventually, don't you worry. People like that don't have the staying power," Eddie responded with a sneer.

"What have you done with all the letters she sent?"

"Put them exactly where they deserve to be – in the bin." Elsie nodded, adding, "I forgot to ask you... When you went through Genevieve's things earlier, had that woman tried to slip anything in there?"

"No, nothing, although I did delete all the pictures from her digital camera of her and that deviant," Eddie said, taking a large gulp of whiskey to quell the rage that was beginning to rise to the surface once more.

"Yes, that was close. I think the main worry we have at the moment is Paul's show. I'm very concerned about that," she said meekly.

"Yes, I know," Eddie said without looking up from his drink. "We'll have to ask Paul what he's intending to do about it."

"Well, I think it's invite only, but that's not very reassuring. In her line of business, she can easily wangle an invitation."

"Then we're going to have to make sure we're with Genevieve every second of the evening. We're not doing such a bad job of keeping them apart now, are we?" he asked triumphantly.

"No, but she may ask more questions about where she lived."

"We'll cross that bridge when we get to it," he said crossly, looking down at his empty glass. "Now, are you going to get me another drink or am I going to have to get out of my chair?"

"Sorry, yes dear," Elsie said as she scurried across the room to the drinks cabinet. They were both startled by the sound of the front door shutting. Laughter echoed through to the living room.

"Mum, Dad, we're back," Genevieve called.

"We're in here, love," Elsie called back whilst refilling Eddie's glass.

The living room door swung open and Genevieve and Paul bounded in.

"Did you have a nice time?" Elsie asked as she sat back down.

"Brilliant!" Genevieve's voice was shrill and threaded with excitement. "We went to the most amazing art show and Paul knew the artist so we all went for drinks afterwards."

"Would you like a drink, Paul?" Eddie asked whilst Genevieve recounted the night's events to

Elsie.

"Whatever you're having, thanks." Elsie went to the drinks cabinet again and poured him a generous amount of whiskey.

"Elsie, why don't you go and rustle up something to eat for these kids?" Eddie asked authoritatively. Elsie got the message and asked Genevieve to help her in the kitchen. When they had gone, Eddie asked Paul to pull up a chair near his.

"Paul, I've got to tell you — I'm pretty concerned about your show." Paul smiled.

"There's nothing to worry about, Eddie."

"But what if she turns up?" he responded tensely.

"I'd be pretty offended if she didn't."

"What!" Eddie bellowed, his face turning scarlet. "Are you insane?"

"Eddie, she's one of the best reviewers in the country, so it would look a bit odd if she wasn't there. In fact, I'm banking on her being there to seal the deal," he said, feeling quite happy with himself.

"What are you going on about?" Eddie said as he started pacing the room.

"I'm not silly enough to think I can keep Genevieve away from her forever. I know there's going to be a time — either now or in the future — when she's going to ask about Rebecca. The more of a mystery she is to her, the more she'll want to find out, so I am going to show her Rebecca and let her see that there is nothing about this woman that she would want or need." Eddie sat down again.

"Isn't that a bit risky Paul? I don't trust that woman. We can't let her get her claws back into her and start warping her mind again."

"Look, Eddie," Paul said, putting his hand on Eddie's shoulder, "if Genevieve was a lesbian," Eddie flinched at the word, "I would be worried, but she's not, and I've managed to get Genevieve to believe in our life together now, so why would I worry about her meeting her again? And anyway, I want her to be there for another reason," he said with a smile.

"What's that?" Eddie asked with a quizzical look on his face.

"I want her to be there when I ask Gen to marry me again."

CHAPTER 14

NEWLY BUILT LUXURY apartments stood next to slick-looking cafés, making the large, grey building on the corner look ugly and out of place. Isabel's office was on the fifth floor, and there was no lift in the building. She'd lost count of how many times she had been up and down the stairs on any given day, but she did know that there were exactly ninety-eight steps until she reached her floor. The stairs wouldn't have been that bad had the final destination been worth it, but it wasn't. A dimly lit corridor with low sagging ceilings led to a small, airless, cluttered office, which she shared with four other officers. Footprints were worn into the old carpets, handprints were smudged on the dreary walls, and the only window in the office was cracked. She'd had to patch it up with masking tape to try to prevent the cold air getting in.

As with the whole building, the office looked like it was on its last legs, in fact she was positive that the conditions they were working under were illegal, but since health inspectors had deemed the place fit for human habitation, there was nothing she could do about it. She'd placed several large plants around the edges of her desk for privacy and long ago managed to block out the dreary conditions. She was grateful her work — it took her out of the office most days — but she was having problems with Genevieve's case.

When it was first assigned to her she thought it would be open and shut, but she could not have been more wrong.

The victim was a lesbian, according to Rebecca, so was it a homophobic attack, was it a mugging, or was it an assault? Despite the police efforts of canvassing the immediate area and a police board stationed where the incident took place, nothing had become known. The only thing she was sure of was that the attack had not been sexual in its nature.

It was unbelievable that no one had seen anything. The embankment should have been busy that morning with tourists and workers alike, but sods law, that stretch just so happened to be empty at the time — either that, or people just weren't coming forward. There were reports of people walking on the street above the embankment hearing loud voices, but in their haste to reach their destination, no one had bothered to look over the wall to see what the commotion was about. There was no physical evidence at the scene that would have pointed Isabel in any direction. Now, two months later, they were no nearer finding the culprit than they were then and she felt the mounting frustration that was always present when she had a case she couldn't close.

While she had been waiting for something to break in the case, she had managed to build a picture of who this woman was through family and friends and, of course, the victim's partner, Rebecca. It was difficult for Isabel to work on a case where her emotions were involved. It had never happened before and she was grateful for this. Seeing Rebecca on a purely friendship basis was not really going against the rules as Rebecca was not a suspect in the case, so she was not really directly involved with it.

Isabel took out Genevieve's file from the cabinet and sat down at her desk. She flicked through it, stopping occasionally to carefully analyse each page as though it was the first time she had seen it. The first few pages were photographs of the crime scene followed by close up images of the injuries Genevieve had sustained. She didn't know whether it was seeing the images again or lack of food that made her stomach feel queasy. It never failed to amaze her that people could hurt someone and just walk off not knowing or caring if that person lived or died. Every new officer to the team was advised that they would get to see the worst side of humanity in the course of their chosen profession and they would get used to it and just move on, but Isabel never did. Each new case shocked her as much as the last one. Whether it was a rape, domestic violence, or anything that involved someone being hurt or killed, it still affected her.

She spread the photographs on her desk, looking intently at them, trying to see if anything was out of place. She carefully analysed the pictures of the crime scene, especially the position where Genevieve had fallen. There wasn't much to go on there. She had been found lying near the pathway wall, blood oozing out of an open wound at the back of her head. It was obvious the attack was deliberate.

Why did Genevieve change the time of her appointment at the last minute? She had to be meeting someone she knew. There were so many questions and the only person who could answer them didn't even know who she was, let alone who had attacked her. Isabel quickly scanned the doctor's report, skipping the medical jargon that went way over her head. What bits she did manage to decipher had to do with the victim's amnesia and the facial injuries she had sustained. There were no other injuries to body; no defence wounds to suggest she had struggled with an assailant.

The forensic report obtained from the Forensic Science Service also offered little in the way of evidence. None of the matter beneath her fingernails had produced a DNA profile other than her own. The spots of blood at the crime scene also all belonged to Genevieve. From the injuries she sustained and the blood on the wall, they concluded that she had been hit in the face, causing her to fall against the wall with a great force. Her laptop had also been forensically analysed. Isabel was always amazed at the advances in technology. Even if someone deleted the hard drive off a machine, it could still be retrieved at a later date using specialist software. In Genevieve's case, there were no emails or messages that showed she was meeting with anyone.

At the time she was discovered she was fully clothed and a valuable necklace still remained around her neck. The last piece of the police report detailed her personal possessions at the time of the attack. Her mobile phone was found in her bag and a log of her calls from the phone company had shown she had only made one call that morning and that was to rearrange her appointment.

There had been some speculation amongst her colleagues that Genevieve's partner had attacked her because she'd found out that she was having an affair.

Although the remarks were made in jest, they were areas that Isabel had had to take into account and investigate. "Everyone is a suspect until they aren't" was her motto. She had quickly managed to rule out Rebecca. She had been investigating Paul as a subject of interest, but was having problems establishing anything worthwhile due to the time of the attack. She knew Genevieve had left Rebecca at around nine-thirty a.m., but the report wasn't called in until around eleven a.m., which meant that there was an hour and a half's time-frame in which anybody could have attacked Genevieve.

When Isabel had visited Paul's home to obtain a statement, she had asked him for an alibi and he had told her he was at home getting ready for his showcase that evening. He said he could account for his whereabouts after eleven-thirty a.m. because he had gone to the gallery for last-minute talks. This was confirmed by the gallery owner. While he couldn't prove that he hadn't done it, she couldn't prove that he had. He'd tried to use his good looks and charm to disarm her, but it hadn't worked, it had just set alarm bells ringing. There was something about his demeanour she didn't like. He had a certain sort of smugness, as though he was relishing every last bit of the drama they were all engulfed in.

She had questioned him about his relationship with Genevieve and he had said that they had once been engaged, but had broken up. He didn't say why they had, which had made her wonder: if he was the victim in this. Why wouldn't he tell her about Genevieve's unfaithfulness and the pain it had caused him? Was it male pride? Or was it because it would give him a motive? Did he think she wouldn't find out? She could just about understand why Genevieve's parents might want to block out her past and push her into a straight life, but she couldn't understand the part he played in it, and more to the point, why he would want any part of it at all.

If Genevieve had left him of her own accord, why would he be so shallow as to try and have a relationship with her when he knew it was not what she would have wanted? Surely if he loved her he would have told her the truth? Every time she had visited Genevieve's parent's house he had been there, all over Genevieve like a rash. It sickened her to see what he was doing, and what was worse was that the parents were actually encouraging him.

She had found out through careful questioning of Genevieve's parents that they had made sure she didn't receive any mail that wasn't vetted first — their excuse was that they didn't want her reading anything which would upset her. They gave the same reason for not having an Internet connection. Papers were carefully selected in case there were any articles about her. Genevieve's father had told Isabel all this information seemingly oblivious to the fact the he had, in essence, encased his daughter in a prison. It was a sorry sight. These were people who professed to love Genevieve, but if that was their idea of love they could keep it.

Two months on and there were no suspects, no leads, and no new evidence. The shrill of the phone beside her startled her and she picked it up immediately.

"Detective Smith," she said. After listening for a

few moments, she continued, "Yes sir, I'll be right there." She gathered up Genevieve's file and headed to her boss's office.

Ted Pikes was a Detective Inspector who had moved through the ranks quickly. He was an amiable man with a perpetual smile. He was sitting behind his desk when Isabel entered his modest office. Not quite as shabby as the rest of the building's interior, its walls were painted a pale green with matching curtains. His glasses were resting in their customary position on his large forehead, which his mop of curly hair failed to conceal.

"Please sit down," he said, motioning for Isabel to sit on the chair opposite him. "So," he began, "how's this Simmons case going?"

"Not very well," she admitted. "There just doesn't seem to be an explanation for it. I've exhausted all avenues and I'm still at a loss." Ted rubbed his eyes and brought his glasses down to rest on his fleshy nose.

"Where do you think this is leading?" he asked, genuinely interested.

"Well sir, until the victim remembers something or we get some new evidence, there isn't much more to be done."

"Well I suggest we put it on the backburner for now, concentrate on your other cases."?"

"Yes sir," she said wearily.

"I'm sure you've tried your best Isabel,"." He saw the dismay in her eyes.

"Don't feel bad about it; we can't get them all the time," he reassured her.

"Thank you, sir." Isabel stood up and went back

to her desk.

CHAPTER 15

CARLA WILLIAMS listened politely and sympathetically to her client charting the destruction of her life in the space of two months. She kept her manicured fingers wrapped around a silver pen, waiting to hear anything of interest that she could note as something to fight back with. What she was hearing did not fill her with great hope. As much as she hated to be the one to do it, she owed it to her client professionally and personally to cut the bullshit and be brutal with the truth. She laid her pen down on the pad of paper and rubbed her forehead, a gesture she used when delivering bad news.

"Rebecca, you don't have a chance in hell. Genevieve is a grown woman who has willingly gone home with her parents. I assume she has the freedom to leave the home as and when she wants to, and she has the free will to pick up the phone and call you should she so wish. It's not a crime to lose your memory and lose contact with people, regardless of how close they were."

Rebecca's heart sank; this was her last attempt to find a way back into Genevieve's life and her hope had been shattered in the space of a few sentences. She stood up wearily and walked over to the window overlooking the Soho shops and bars. For what seemed like an age to Carla, Rebecca stood still as a statue, gazing straight ahead, seemingly indifferent to the hustle and bustle of life on the streets below. Carla stood up and walked over to join Rebecca, putting her arm around her shoulders.

"You will get through this." That was something she didn't say lightly. She'd had clients in worse emotional states than Rebecca whom she thought had no chance of surviving, but she had been proven wrong time and time again when they had walked back through her office door like new people. Knowing Rebecca as she did, she knew she would overcome this situation, whichever way it turned out.

"If — and it's a big if — her parents try to start interfering in her financial matters," she began to say, feeling Rebecca stiffen in her grip, "we will have more leeway to act. We could then make the truth about your relationship public, which makes me think that they are in no rush to cut ties with you completely... not yet anyway. But," she said, rubbing her arm, "hopefully Genevieve's memory will have come back by the time anything that drastic happens."

Rebecca slowly let out a heavy breath and turned to look at her solicitor.

"This is what happens when you take things for granted, isn't it," she said with a hint of finality. Carla released her arm from around Rebecca's shoulders; there was nothing more she could say. Rebecca gave her a quick kiss on her cheek and thanked her for her time.

"I'll be there with you every step of the way," Carla called out to Rebecca as she left her office.

Emerging from the air conditioned building, Rebecca was assaulted by the heat that engulfed her like a blanket as she stood on the pavement. She took off her cardigan and opened the top few buttons on her blouse to find some relief from the oppressive air. Almost as if she was on autopilot, she began walking in the direction of the underground. Once there, she found herself buying a ticket and making her way to the platform. She was grateful that it wasn't rush hour and there weren't many people around. With the sound of the rattling train approaching fast, she waited for it to come into view. She imagined for one split second that she could just end all this pain there and then. All it would take would be to put one foot over the edge and it would all be blissfully over.

Coming to her senses, she took a couple of steps back as the train came to a screeching halt in front of her and waited for the few passengers to make their way off before boarding the claustrophobic carriage. She often wondered how on earth people used the underground to go to work. All packed in like cattle, strangers' bodies pressed close together, breathing in the same stale air. The very thought of it just made her shudder. She was relieved when she changed at Victoria from the underground to an overhead train to Surrey.

When she reached her destination, she took a taxi from the station to Genevieve's parents' house. Her mind echoed with the sound of Peter warning her to stay away from there, but she couldn't help herself, she was desperate. She asked the taxi driver to stop halfway down the street and she made the rest of the journey on foot, stopping to hide behind a large oak tree opposite the house. She peeked out, looking for any signs of movement and drew her head back quickly when the lights in the front room went on.

Slowly, she moved out to look into the room. She could make out all four figures standing there, their movements indicating they were sharing a joke. She knew she was torturing herself, but she couldn't turn away. She had to see this for herself. It was true, what Carla had said, Genevieve was there of her own accord, and as much as it hurt Rebecca to admit it, she looked quite happy.

She shifted uncomfortably on her feet to ease the discomfort in her leg muscles as they began to ache from standing in the same position for too long. She hadn't even noticed that the daylight was giving way to darkness. She also hadn't noticed the drop in the temperature until she began to feel chilly. She wrapped her arms around herself and tried to generate some heat.

The living room light went off and she assumed they had left the room. She was just about to leave the cover of the tree when the front door opened and the laughter of Genevieve filtered through the air. It was soon joined by Paul's and followed by goodbyes and then the door slamming shut. She peeked round the tree again to see Genevieve and Paul walking down the pathway together like childhood sweethearts. He paused to snap off a red rose from the rose bush that grew in the front garden and handed it to her gallantly. She took it and played along with him by curtseying.

They both burst out laughing and made their way to a parked car. Once inside, she managed to catch one last glimpse of the happy couple before they drove off, and it was one that broke her heart. Paul leaned over and kissed Genevieve on the lips.

Rebecca couldn't bear to watch what happened next. The thought of having to see Genevieve embrace him was too much for her and she ran alone into the night, pins and needles shooting through her unused legs; the sound of her thumping heart drowning out the thoughts that were trying to consume her.

CHAPTER 16

REBECCA DIALLED the number from the piece of paper she held in her hand. The phone was answered after six rings. She spoke three words:

"Dinner, my treat." Upon hearing the reply she smiled and hung up. Two hours later she stood on the corner of Dean Street waiting for her dinner date. When she arrived, the two women embraced and walked toward their chosen restaurant in Chinatown.

Once seated and having placed their orders, Rebecca began, "I hope you don't mind me calling?"

"Of course not; that's why I gave you my number," Isabel said, smiling. Rebecca shifted in her seat and then asked

"So, how have you been since our last night out?"

"Let's just say I never thought I would recover... I'm not as young as I used to be! It took me two days for that hangover to work through," Isabel replied.

Rebecca laughed.

"I know what you mean; I didn't fare that well either. Can you imagine there was a time when we didn't really care about hangovers? Now I have to weigh up how much damage each glass of wine will do to me."

"Well, Tia was the lucky one." Then Isabel quickly added, "To escape the hangover, that is."

"Even if she hadn't gone home early she still

wouldn't have been ill. I don't think in all the years I've known her that I've ever seen her ill after a night out. She's the person that everyone envies the day after," Rebecca said, smiling while reminiscing.

"How is she?"

"She's fine. I think you have an admirer." Isabel blushed.

"She's very nice, but..."

"Not in that way," Rebecca said, smiling.

"That's an over-used cliché isn't it?"

"Not really; you can't help who you're attracted to, and anyway, you two aren't suited."

"And why is that?" Isabel asked, leaning forward.

"Well, for starters, you're a police officer."

"And?"

"And I don't think you would quite appreciate some of Tia's, shall we say... habits?"

"Say no more," Isabel said, holding up her hand jokingly. "If you could find me a woman who doesn't have... ahem, ahem... certain habits, I'd eat my non-existent hat."

"Well, you'd better start eating it," Rebecca replied playfully.

"You?" She nodded. "I can quite believe it."

"Hey, what does that mean? Do you think I look straight laced?" she said, feigning insult.

"No, just sensible," Isabel replied, trying not to smile too broadly.

"Lucky escape."

The food was brought to their table and they ate hungrily, both women realising that they hadn't eaten since lunch time. Isabel knew she had to tell Rebecca that she was no longer actively working on the case, but didn't quite know how to break it to her.

"Would you like to go for a drink somewhere quiet?" Isabel asked.

"Sounds serious."

Isabel was hesitant, choosing her words carefully. "It's just something you need to know about the case."

Rebecca studied Isabel's face and signalled for the waiter so she could settle the bill. The women made their way to a pub around the corner from the restaurant in silence. The stench of stale alcohol assaulted their senses as they walked through the door. Rebecca thought again that maybe having non-smoking bars wasn't such a good idea — at least the smoke covered the odour!

The pub was close enough to deserted, just a few men drinking their beers, watching the large TV screen showing football and occasionally yelling out an obscenity when their team failed to score. Rebecca went to the bar while Isabel found them a table.

"What can I get you?" the disinterested bar attendant asked. Her jet black hair matched the colour of her eye liner, pencilled so thickly around her eyes that they nearly disappeared, and her hook nose made Rebecca think of a raven.

"Two white wines please," she answered, matching her tone of voice. The bar attendant sloppily poured the drinks into two wine glasses, splashing it over the sides.

"Eight quid," she said. Rebecca laid a ten pound note on the bar, picked up her drinks and walked away. She'd spent more than enough time in the raven's company. She caught sight of where Isabel was and walked toward her, grateful she had chosen to sit as far away from the bar and that woman's bad vibes as possible.

"So what's the bad news?" Rebecca asked, sitting down.

"There's no easy way to tell you so I will just say it... I'm no longer working on Genevieve's case."

"Okay," Rebecca said slowly, not quite understanding why this would cause a problem. She sipped her wine slowly and pulled a face as the alcohol hit her taste buds.

"I don't think you understand. Neither I nor anyone else will be working her case anymore."

"What!" Rebecca was taken aback, her face aghast. "What do you mean, no one will be working her case? Are you trying to tell me you're closing it?" Her eyes narrowed.

"In a way, yes. If we get any new evidence we will reopen it, but for now there's no more I can do. I've tried, Rebecca; I've gone down every road I can think of trying to find something, but everywhere I turn I'm met with a dead end. I'm really sorry," she said. Rebecca held her head in both hands, shaking it.

"This can't be happening! What about Paul?" she said, clutching at straws in desperation. "Even you said yourself that it was suspicious that the invitation just so happened to turn up out of the blue the day Genie was attacked."

"Yes, I know, but I've got nothing on him. There's nothing that links him to being there that morning — no DNA — nothing. Short of him coming to the station and making a full confession, he's done nothing wrong, and if he has, I can't find the evidence."

"So that's it then," Rebecca said softly, more to herself. "That's how the story ends."

"Rebecca, if I get the slightest whiff of information that could shed new light on this case I will be all over it, but until then..." Isabel shrugged her shoulders, defeated. Rebecca sipped her wine and let out a long sigh.

"This nightmare is never going to end; there's never going to be any closure."

"Rebecca, you have to have hope. Genevieve is still alive and if her memory recovers, and it was Paul who was responsible, we'll nail the bastard — that I can promise you."

She leaned over and squeezed Rebecca's shoulder, trying to reassure her but knowing full well how futile her statement was. Rebecca shook her head as though disagreeing with herself — she just couldn't believe that whoever had hurt Genevieve was going to get away with it.

"I need some fresh air," she said, pushing her unfinished glass of wine towards the middle of the table. As they made their way to the exit, Isabel touched her shoulder lightly.

"Look, why don't you come to my place for a while?" Rebecca hesitated for a fraction of a second, and then nodded — anywhere was better than going home and being alone right now.

Surprisingly, they didn't live that far apart. Isabel's home was a flat in a converted house in Elephant and Castle. Though for many years the council had proclaimed that the area was under renovation, Rebecca still couldn't see any changes evident. Shop fronts still looked worn, their metal shutters covered with graffiti. Large office blocks and houses alike were covered in discoloured paint, peeling from the brickwork it had once stuck to. Isabel asked the taxi driver to turn off the main road onto a quiet residential street. Rebecca was surprised to see the row of houses standing neatly next to each other.

Out of the chaos comes order, she thought to herself. The outside of the houses were obviously maintained as the paint looked fresh, hedges were trimmed and there wasn't a scrap of rubbish to be seen. Isabel paid the taxi driver and led Rebecca into a house. Her flat was one of six leading off a communal hall. Fresh lilies stood on a table in the middle of it with envelope holders for each of the flat's mail. The hardwood floor was polished, with a multi-coloured rug lying in the middle of it, adding to its welcoming feel. Isabel's flat was small, but not cramped. The passageway led to a light and airy front room. The wine-red walls were lightened by the furniture and wooden blinds and a small fireplace occupied the centre of a wall, wood logs built up inside the grate. A large beige sofa by the window and an oak coloured coffee table in front of it finished the scene. It seemed that Isabel was very well organised — nothing looked out of place. The room had a warm, lived-in feel about it, but Rebecca couldn't help noticing the distinct lack of a personal presence. Isabel had no knick-knacks or personal photographs on display. Her home revealed nothing about herself — which was just the way she was herself. Rebecca hadn't failed to notice that Isabel rarely, if ever talked about herself, and she had never once mentioned having a partner — present or past.

"White wine okay?" Isabel asked Rebecca, who nodded. "Make yourself at home," she said as she left the room. Once alone Rebecca headed straight for the large bookcase, complete with crime books and biographies of homicide profilers. She turned round when she heard Isabel enter the room.

"I see you don't like light reading," Rebecca said, nodding toward the book shelf.

"Actually, if you had taken the time to look at the bottom row you would have seen my collection of Mills and Boon."

Rebecca looked at her with disbelief.

"I'm not joking," she said, "look for yourself." Rebecca bent down and saw she was telling the truth. Amongst all the books about murder and crime sat soppy romantic tales.

"Well I would never have guessed," Rebecca said, crossing the room and sitting on the large sofa.

"That's one of the first things you learn in my line of work... looks can be deceiving." She handed her a glass of wine and they clinked each other's glasses. The front room door creaked open and a small form wandered into the room.

"Aah, and here's the man of the house," Isabel said as her cat jumped onto the sofa. She stroked his black and white fur fondly. "Rebecca, meet Manson." The cat purred, responding to the strokes he was receiving. He lay on his back, waiting for his belly to be rubbed.

"Wow, he sure knows what he likes," Rebecca said as the cat wiggled his body ecstatically. He had black patches around his eyes, giving the impression that he was wearing a mask, and his small pink mouth curved as though he was smiling. He reminded Rebecca of the joker from Batman. "He's beautiful... and the largest, most muscular cat I have ever seen! How long have you had him?"

"Three years," she said, still stroking Manson. "I was working on a case where the victim worked in a cat shelter. I went along to take a statement from her colleagues and as I was leaving this little one caught my eye — didn't you?" she said, switching to baby talk with the cat. "I just knew there and then that I couldn't leave him there, so the next day I went and collected him and he's been my partner-in-crime ever since!"

"And what about any other partners?" Rebecca asked as she joined in stroking the cat. Isabel turned to look out the window. "I'm sorry if you think I'm prying," she said.

"No, you're not prying," Isabel said slowly. It was obvious from her demeanour that she was troubled by her thoughts. "It's just one of those silly scenarios that every gay woman swears she'll never find herself in, but eventually always does." She got up and walked over to the fireplace, bending over to light the wood with a box of matches. The kindling caught fire almost immediately. She stood up and looked at Rebecca, pain etched on her face.

"I swore blind I would never talk about this, but I think you can relate to what it feels like to lose someone." She picked her drink up from the table. "I met Amy through friends of mine — they all knew I was a sucker for hard-done-by women, and she fitted the mould perfectly. They warned me away from her, but I wouldn't listen — too caught up in my 'saviour mode.' She'd been having trouble with her boyfriend and I suggested she stay with me until it all blew over. We became lovers. One week turned into one month, then a year. We were pretty committed to one another, though I always had that fear in the back of my mind that she'd go back to a man."

She shrugged.

"Well, it seemed that my fear was unfounded when she suggested we have a baby and settle down as a family. God, I couldn't believe my luck, everything I had ever wanted was now coming true! We decided that she should be the one that got pregnant...." She paused, shaking her head. "Oh, it was going to be so simple; we find a man; get him checked out; get his sperm; she has the baby and we live happily ever after...." She laughed bitterly.

"Well, it all went according to plan alright. We found the donor — an old friend of hers who was eager to help us out. He was fine about not having any rights or playing any part in bringing the baby up when it was born, so..." She sighed. "Everything was set and ready to go, he played his part to the T, always having the sperm available whenever the previous attempts had failed. Anyway, we had success after a couple of months, and before we knew it we had a new baby at home. You should have seen this place, it looked like mother care!"

She smiled at the memory, and then it vanished from her face. "Out of the blue, Amy soon decided that her friend should be able to see the baby — after all, it was his child, she said... I couldn't believe it, but went along with it because it meant so much to her. Anyway, one visit turned into two, and then three, and then he was always round here. Amy and I fought non-stop, which wasn't good for the baby, and in the end we broke up. She moved out to her parents — or so I thought. Turns out she moved in with him." She dropped her head, afraid she might start to cry. "I later found out that the baby was conceived the natural way."

Rebecca was at a loss for words. Silence hung in the air like a heavy cloak. Isabel leaned over to the table to refill her drink. She'd managed to convince herself she was over it, but it clearly still hurt.

"And there you have it," she said, raising her glass to Rebecca.

"When was the last time you saw her?" she asked sympathetically.

"Oh, not so long ago; she and her husband and child." Rebecca gasped.

"She married him?" Isabel smiled bitterly again.

"Oh yes, and now it's just me and Manson — and I wouldn't have it any other way." As if on cue Manson jumped down from the sofa, stretched and walked over to Isabel, lying down in front of her. She picked him up and held him in her arms like a baby, stroking underneath his chin, which he seemed to like as he made no attempt to escape.

"This isn't how it's meant to be, is it?" Rebecca said, smiling sadly. "Whatever happened to all of the 'happily ever after' endings?" she said, nodding in the direction of the Mills and Boon books on the shelf.

"Yeah, well, we can all dream. Anyway, are you feeling better now?" Isabel asked abruptly.

"If you want the honest answer, no, I'm not alright. I'm tired... I'm tired of how tough life is, I'm tired of the shit people bring into my life, I'm tired of waiting for the pain to go away, which it doesn't."

Isabel took the wine glass out of Rebecca's hand and put both glasses on the table.

"Come here," she said, drawing Rebecca into her arms and stroking her hair as though she was a child. Rebecca began to cry all the tears that she had held in because she was too afraid to let go of them; scared that if they fell she would be admitting it was the end, that Genevieve really wasn't coming back. She felt a strange comfort being in Isabel's arms. It was the first time in years that she had been this close to a woman other than Genevieve. She felt Isabel planting little kisses on the top of her head and rocking her gently from side to side. Though it was an intimate gesture, there was nothing sexual in the embrace — and yet Rebecca felt a little deceitful.

She gently eased her way out of Isabel's arms.

"I'm sorry," she said. "I'm not normally so emotional."

"You don't have to apologise to me for feeling hurt Rebecca. I don't know what I would do in your shoes." Isabel picked up their wine glasses and handed one to Rebecca and took a long mouthful of her own. She hoped that Rebecca could not hear her heart thumping. She had never felt like this before and the worst thing was Rebecca could never and would never feel the same way about her. She watched her mentally get herself together, making small talk with Isabel, trying to play down her loss of control. She wondered if she was always so controlled or had Genevieve been able to break though the armour she wore around herself. Isabel made a conscious decision that night: She would be a friend to Rebecca for as long as she needed her and would put her own feelings on the back burner for now. If Genevieve got her memory back, all well and good, but if she didn't...

CHAPTER 17

GENEVIEVE HAD BEEN enjoying the sessions with her counsellor. It was the only place where she could really tell the truth.

"So, how are you feeling today?" her counsellor asked, clasping her pale white bloodless hands together.

"Restless. It's always the same: I feel caged in that house; I feel like my parents are looking at every move I make."

"How are your feelings toward Paul?" She leaned back, settling her heavy bulk comfortably into the leather chair, squishing noises matching her every move.

Genevieve blushed.

"I don't know. I can imagine that I would be attracted to someone like him, but..."

"But?" Dr Covette asked, her thick eyebrows meeting together in a frown, her wide gazing eyes conveying years of wisdom.

"It's just not in here," she said putting her hand on her stomach. "He doesn't reach me... Oh, I can't explain it!"

"Yes you can, just take your time."

"Okay, I just don't feel the connection that I feel there should be...." She looked around the office, which she had sat in for the past few weeks. Stark white walls and minimalist furnishings gave the illusion that the office was bigger than it was.

"Do you feel a connection with anyone else?"

"Only my work," Genevieve said bluntly.

"So, no human connection so far?"

"No. Don't get me wrong — I like him and think he's incredibly talented but —"

"You just don't connect," the counsellor said solemnly.

"What about friends from the art world — do you feel any connection with them?"

"I don't know. I haven't met any of them yet, though I did meet a woman who said she was my flatmate," Genevieve replied enthusiastically.

"And?"

"And I liked her very much... Well I must have done, because I shared a flat with her."

"So why haven't you seen her? Surely you need to be around as many people as you know to give you a breadth of knowledge about who you are?" the counsellor asked, her soothing voice probing further.

"My parents don't like her — and neither does Paul. And as far as I know, she hasn't tried to contact me. None of my friends have," Genevieve responded bitterly.

"Do you know why your parents and Paul don't like her?"

"No."

"Have you ever asked them why?"

Genevieve sighed. "I've tried to, but they get irritable when they even hear her name. They more or less threw her out of the hospital when I was there."

"Was she acting badly?"

"Not at all, but I couldn't remember who she was, so my dad told her to leave."

"Has Paul talked about her?"

"God no, just the mere mention of her name makes him tense!" Dr Covette raised her eyebrows.

"Frankly Genevieve, it sounds like there's a lot more to this than meets the eye. You know you lived somewhere else, but so far no-one has offered to take you back there to see if it has any effect on your memory. Which then begs the question: What do you think is more important, pleasing your parents and Paul, or trying to get your memory back?"

"Obviously getting my memory back, but at the same time I don't want to upset my family. This must be hard enough as it is for them."

"But what about you? Isn't it hard for you, not remembering? Genevieve, I'm not here to upset the apple cart, but I am here to help you with your memory loss, and I believe it imperative that you remember all aspects of your life — not just a select few. It sounds to me as if they're hiding things from you. They may have good intentions at heart, but you need to be reminded of as many details in your past as possible if you are to have any hope of recovery."

Genevieve put her head back on the couch for a few seconds, fighting the tears back. She knew that if she left her parents' home it would break their hearts, but what the doctor had said was true. How was she ever going to find herself if she was only being shown one side of her life? Her counsellor sat quietly while Genevieve battled with her mind.

"Would you like a tissue?"

"No, thank you."

Genevieve looked up at the clock — just five minutes to go. She felt sad as she sat there. She was sad that she would never see Dr Covette again and even worse that she was going to have to break her parents' hearts. She was going home, to wherever home was. She hoped Rebecca wouldn't mind her moving back in, but she had to find out what was going on. She would tell Paul and her parents after he had exhibited his work.

* * *

Arriving home, Genevieve walked through the front door, straight into a box in the hallway.

Is this the sum total of my previous life? One box?

"Hey, you're here," Paul said, appearing from behind them. He reached for her and held her in a hug. "Shall I take this up to your room?"

"I'll just take my camera with me for the minute," she said. He opened the box and sifted through until he found what she wanted.

"Aah, here it is," he said, handing her the box.

"Thanks. I think I'm going to lay down for a bit."

"Okay, I'll see you later then," he said, pecking her on the cheek. "I'll just say goodbye to your parents and I'll be off."

Ever since she'd been to his flat for dinner, he'd been visiting her every day and her parents seemed happy to encourage him. A drunken kiss had been as much as she could offer him that night, even though he'd tried his hardest to get her to change her mind. She had pacified him by saying she wanted to take things slowly and that she was sure everything would be right between them again. He had seemed happy enough with this and had taken her home when she asked.

She went up to her bedroom and put the box on the bed. Opening the box, and taking out her camera, she examined it from all angles. She didn't recognise it as her own but she liked the look and feel of it. She opened the viewing lens to flick through the pictures that were stored on it. They didn't trigger any memories; anybody could have taken them. She slumped down on the bed and felt her stomach churn. She had a whole life out there somewhere, just waiting to be claimed, and she'd be damned if she was just going to live the rest of her life waiting for someone to bring her the clues she needed! In that instant, she knew that the decision she'd made in the counsellor's office was the right one. How her parents and Paul were going to take the news about her leaving she didn't know, but she did know one thing: She was definitely going.

CHAPTER 18

DRESSED IN A FLAWLESSLY cut charcoal grey suit and crisp white shirt, Paul thought of the evening ahead. It was at The Ivy House that his life had begun its downward spiral. The memory rekindled the old feelings of hate, bitterness and resentment. His thoughts darkened, as if a black cloud had spread across them. He fought to pull himself up from the cold depths of despair.

"That was then, this is now," he told himself firmly, "and everything is going according to plan." He tapped the ring in his pocket just to make sure it was still there. It was the same ring he had given to Genevieve all those years ago, only this time he was going to make sure she didn't get away.

Whiteness powdered the blue sky, the first patters of rain beginning to drop. The weather forecast had predicted heavy rain but that didn't stop people making their way in droves into The Ivy House art gallery. Large black umbrellas plodded along like a procession as people made their way into the building. The car with Paul and his party of supporters pulled up next to the kerb outside the gallery. Not bothering to use an umbrella, they quickly walked the short distance to the modern, glass-fronted building.

As Paul pushed open the large glass door, he tried to brush off the memories that were trying to invade his mind again. He was grateful when he caught sight of the gallery owner and went over to greet him.

"Paul," Bill, the owner said, his deeply lined faced breaking into a smile revealing perfectly straight teeth. He shook his hand enthusiastically before turning his plump, well-dressed body to Genevieve.

"Genevieve," he said, taking her hand to his lips, "a pleasure to see you again."

"You too," she replied, forcing a smile through the unwanted intimate contact. She had no idea who he was.

"I'm sure you remember Genevieve's parents, Eddie and Elsie," Paul said.

"Of course," Bill replied, placing his hand into Eddie's firm handshake and briefly acknowledging Elsie with a smile. "Nice to see you all again," he said, looking at them all with one sweeping gaze.

"Well, Paul," he said, turning his attention back to him, "looks like a full house tonight." He beamed. "Some of the big fish are here, let's just hope we can reel them in," he said, nudging Paul with his elbow. Paul smiled politely.

"Well, I'd better get in there, then," he said, taking Genevieve's hand in his.

"I'll see you later," Bill said as he welcomed a handsome couple coming through the door.

Paul led Genevieve and her parents into the main hall where his exhibit was being held. He paused at the doorway for a moment, drinking in the noise, the crowd, and the buzz of excitement. He was buoyed up by the scene. His paintings, which once leaned up against his studio's walls, now hung on large white walls, the new setting making them look larger than life.

"You've done yourself proud," Eddie said, placing a firm hand on Paul's shoulder.

"Yes, you have," Elsie said meekly, feeling inadequate in her conservative grey suit compared to the glamorous-looking women and well-heeled men who littered the hall. She deplored her own insecurities, but she couldn't overcome them, no matter how hard she tried. A weary feeling of acceptance fell over her as she stood by Eddie's side.

He, in comparison, looked as though he was the star of the show. He was like a chameleon — he could quite easily adapt to any situation.

"I'll get Elsie and myself a drink, why don't you two go off and socialise and catch up with us later," Eddie said.

Paul wrapped his arm around Genevieve's waist as a gesture of ownership and walked into the throng of people. Her outward tranquillity hid an inward tremor of uncertainty. People were saying her name in a very familiar tone, but she didn't recognise any of them. All she could do was smile at them uneasily and be grateful when they moved on. She couldn't help but feel that people were discussing her rather than Paul's art.

They were stopped several more times whilst Paul spoke to people as they made their way slowly to the area where he was going to make an opening speech. He walked up the stairs to the makeshift stage and someone in the crowd yelled, "Quiet please!"

The room quietened down and Paul stood there

under the bright light, feeling like a king among men. This was his time. He thanked everybody for attending, gave a brief background on why art was so important to him, and finished his speech by talking about the inspiration behind the paintings. He held his glass up in the air.

"To Gen, without whom none of this would have been possible." The crowd echoed, "To Gen."

She stood rooted to the floor while everyone around her clapped and smiled and Paul made his way back down the steps to join her. She wished the floor would swallow her up.

Genevieve wasn't the only one wishing she was somewhere else. Rebecca was standing to the side of stage and had a clear view of Genevieve. She found it hard to tear her gaze away. Genevieve's vulnerability made her appear even more appealing. Rebecca longed to touch her, to look into her eyes and see the warmth and love that she once held there for her. The intensity of her longing was amplified by the fact that Genevieve's parents and Paul had literally built a wall around her. She recalled the words of the poet, Luke Davies, who they both loved. The words described how they felt when apart from each other: "Desire can occur in the brain, the mind, as well as elsewhere, whereas longing, true yearning, tends to bypass the rational centres and take place in the limbs. It's even beyond the heart, quite possibly."

She was brought back to reality by Tia, who looked like she was about to explode.

"I can't do this, Becca — I really can't. I'm going to have to say something." She started to walk away but Rebecca grabbed her arm.

"That's not the way. She won't even know who you are. Can you imagine if it was the other way around, and someone who you didn't know approached you and started ranting in public that you were a lesbian?" Tia smiled.

"Yes, I can see how that would pose a bit of a problem."

"And you'd probably be thrown out for making a nuisance of yourself. It's a good thing you know people in high places," Isabel said, standing behind Tia. Tia swung around and embraced her.

"What are you doing here?" she asked

"I invited her," Rebecca said offering her cheek to Isabel.

"And in what capacity are you here, may I ask?" Tia said, raising one eyebrow.

"Personal, but that's not to say I won't be on the lookout," she said and winked at Rebecca.

Rebecca and Tia felt dejected as they stood looking in the direction of Genevieve and Paul.

"Well, one thing we can do," Tia said, taking three glasses of champagne from the waiter's tray in both hands, "is get drunk." She handed Isabel a glass, but before she could hand one to Rebecca, the critic shook her head.

"No, that's not the way either," Rebecca said tersely, suddenly overcome with anger. She'd had enough playing by everyone else's rules. She walked through the crowd until she came to the small group where Paul was standing with Genevieve.

"There you are," she said brightly to Genevieve, edging past Paul. "I heard you were going to be here tonight." She reached over to kiss Genevieve's cheek and thought she was going to cry when her lips made contact. She noted that the woman she loved no longer wore her favourite perfume. She stood back, taking in the whole view of Genevieve.

"You look very well," was all she allowed herself to say, feeling the presence of Paul's glare.

"Thank you," Genevieve replied, her cheeks flushed, embarrassed by Rebecca's familiarity. Rebecca turned to Paul, ignoring the disdain on his face.

"Paul, tonight is obviously going to be a great success; you have really excelled yourself this time." She smiled through gritted teeth. "I'm sure you won't mind if I steal Genevieve away for a few moments," she said, taking Genevieve by the arm. "An old friend wants to see her," she said sweetly, leading Genevieve away. The colour drained from Paul's face as he stood there with his mouth open, unable to form a sentence.

Rebecca guided Genevieve through the crowd to where Tia and Isabel stood. Tia looked on at her, amazed. She couldn't believe she had just literally stolen Genevieve from under Paul's nose. Tia could tell immediately by the way Genevieve looked at her that she didn't recognise her. *What a cruel world this is*, she thought to herself.

"Genevieve, this is Tia, an old friend of yours. You wouldn't believe it to look at her, but you used to follow some of her pretty bad ways," Rebecca joked.

"She's lying!" Tia feigned innocence and embraced Genevieve. Like Rebecca, the sadness of the situation made her feel like crying. She squeezed her tightly before letting her go, Genevieve's face revealing her uneasiness. Her name or face didn't ring any bells to Genevieve.

"Hi," was all she could say. She looked over her shoulder to see where Paul was and found him staring hard at her. She couldn't read his face, and wasn't sure if he was angry with her, but he certainly didn't look pleased. She smiled at him and he smiled tensely back. She returned her attention to the women.

"And you remember Detective Smith?" Rebecca continued.

"Isabel, please," she said, shaking Genevieve's hand.

"Hello again." She didn't know who to speak to first. All eyes were on her and she was at a loss of what to say. Turning to Tia she said awkwardly, "So you were responsible for leading me astray, were you?"

"Maybe it's a good thing you can't remember," she said jokingly, then put her hand to her mouth. "I'm sorry, that was in poor taste." Genevieve smiled.

"It's fine; it's nice to be treated normally."

"So you really can't remember anything — not Rebecca, not your flat, job...?" Tia asked, encouraged by what she saw as an open opportunity to try and jog her friend's memory.

"I'm afraid not. I know my work instinctively, but as for everything else — no."

While Genevieve was talking with Tia, Isabel was watching Rebecca. The expression on Rebecca's face spoke volumes and how Genevieve could not see how madly and utterly in love Rebecca was with her, she didn't know. *She really must be straight*, Isabel thought. All Rebecca needed to do to complete the picture of a love-sick puppy was to start drooling. The hunger in her eyes was undeniable.

"So is Paul helping you put two and two together?" Tia's voice broke into Isabel's thoughts.

"He tries his best, but so far no luck. It's very frustrating not being able to remember anything about him."

"It must be awful for him," Tia muttered under her breath, smiling sweetly at Genevieve.

"I haven't seen you since I came out of the hospital," Genevieve said to Rebecca, feeling herself blush under her scrutiny.

"No, I thought it best to wait for you to settle down first," she lied.

"Oh, right." The conversation tailed off into a painful silence.

"So anyway," Tia said, aware that no one else was going to steer the conversation to where they really wanted it to be, "does this gallery look familiar in any way to you?" Genevieve shook her head. "You had your first break here. This is where your career took off, not to mention your friendship with Rebecca," she said nodding toward her.

"I know I had a showcase here, but I didn't know this was where I met you," Genevieve said to Rebecca.

"Yes, in fact..." Tia was on a roll, but before she had a chance to complete her sentence, Paul had appeared at Genevieve's side, all charming and handsome, like butter wouldn't melt in his mouth.

"Sorry to interrupt you ladies," he said, taking hold of Genevieve's hand. "I'm sure you've still got lots to talk about, but Gen, there are some people I would really like you to meet."

"Okay, well it was nice to see you all. Hopefully we'll catch up later," Genevieve just managed to say before Paul dragged her away from them.

He led her out into the spacious foyer.

"So, what were you talking about?" he enquired, his eyes fixed on the floor.

"Nothing in particular, just about my memory loss really."

"You all seemed to be pretty pally," he said.

"Paul, why wouldn't I be pally with them if they were my friends?"

"You'll just have to take my word for it that you are better off without those two."

"Says who?" she demanded to know.

"Look, let's not have a scene here," he said, looking around him.

"A scene?" she asked in a hushed, angry voice. "Is this is a scene? You drag me away from my friends and then tell me I'm better off without them! To tell you the truth, Paul, I'm getting pretty pissed off with all these secrets that I feel are being kept from me."

"There are no secrets," he said, getting worried that he'd pushed her too far. "I'm sorry, it's just nerves."

"No Paul, I don't believe it is because of your nerves. I want to know the truth. What is it about Rebecca that you and my parents don't like?" She stood there with her hands on her hips — her body language telling him he was not going to get out of this easily.

"How about I tell you the whole story later? Now really isn't the time."

"Paul, at the moment, all I have to go on is what you're telling me and I'm hoping that putting my trust in you is not being abused in any way."

"Of course not, darling," he said, shepherding her back toward the gallery. "If you don't trust what I say, you only have to ask your parents..." he added.

* * *

An hour later, Genevieve stood out on the small balcony to get some fresh air. Paul had been cornered by some VIPs and her parents were basking in the glory of his success. She breathed in the cool evening air.

"Hot in there, isn't it?" a by-now familiar voice said behind her. She turned sideways to see Rebecca.

"Yes, not to mention my aching feet," she said, lifting up her foot to show off her high heels.

"You always insisted on wearing heels even when you knew you had a long night ahead of you," Rebecca said softly.

There was not much of a gap between them and without Paul present, something about the close proximity felt comforting to Genevieve.

"In that case, it's true that old habits die hard."

"Yes, they do." Looking directly into Genevieve's eyes, the smile faded from Rebecca's face. She ventured, "I miss you." Genevieve didn't know what to say.

"Was I that good a flatmate?"

"Yes, you were." She put her hand to Genevieve's

face. "You've got an eyelash on your cheek," she said, removing it slowly, savouring the contact. Both women's eyes were locked onto one another. Neither spoke — in that moment, it was as if just the two of them existed. Genevieve felt glued to the floor and couldn't move. There was something so intimate about the moment that it made her blush. Rebecca took her hand and put the eyelash in it.

"Make a wish," she said, closing her hand into a ball and reluctantly letting go. Genevieve closed her eyes and after a few seconds opened them.

"Let's hope it comes true," she said, smiling sadly.

In that moment Rebecca knew in her heart that she could not simply blurt out who she was to her. She knew it wouldn't be fair to Genevieve, not because of her parents or Paul, but because she didn't want to add to the confusion she could see Genevieve going through. She could see her mentally fighting to understand what was going on between them and it wasn't up to her to shatter Genevieve's world. Regretfully, she turned to go back inside.

"I hope we can stay in touch, Genie," was all she said as she walked away without a backward glance.

* * *

"Paul you're a star," a drunken blonde slurred in Paul's ear. Her flimsy black dress was in real danger of exposing her large attributes and she was flirting outrageously with him. She was flattering him with comments about his artwork and how she could open doors for him in the art world. His focus, however, was on the balcony. Paul had seen the exchange between Rebecca and Genevieve and had frozen in fear when he saw Rebecca reach up and touch Genevieve's face. His fear turned to anger as they both stood motionless, looking into each other's eyes. He couldn't let Rebecca do this to him again. He had waited patiently, using all of his willpower not to go and drag Rebecca away from her. When she eventually left the balcony he went out there to join Genevieve.

"You okay?" he asked.

"Yes, of course. Are you having a good time?"

"The best," he beamed, "and having you by my side makes it all the more special, Gen." She was afraid to meet his eyes in case of what he'd see.

"I love you, Gen."

"I know you do," she replied, keeping her gaze averted.

"But you still can't say it to me, can you?" She didn't answer. There was an unbearable silence between them. "You know your parents are getting pretty anxious about where we're heading?" he said, trying a different angle. "In fact, I would go so far as to say that they're disappointed by the lack of progress we've made."

"This is not about my parents, Paul."

"No, no it's not; it's about us, it's about you and me, and it's about me losing the only person I have ever loved to something I can't compete with. I can't compete with your mind Gen, because it has more power over you than I do. I love you and I want this to work, I really do, but I can't do it on my own. You once told me I was your life — was that a lie?"

"I don't know."

"Oh come on," he said irritably, "get off the fence and make a decision, do you want me or not?" This was his last big gamble. He was relying on her sense of fair play to make the decision for her.

"Well, do you?" He pulled out the diamond ring from his pocket and got down on his knee. "Do you want to be my wife?"

"Um... yes?" she said hesitantly.

"You won't regret this Gen, you really won't." He embraced her tightly, kissed her briefly, and then grabbed her hand, taking her through the door. He hurriedly made his way to the makeshift stage with her struggling to keep up with him in her heels. Jumping on stage with energy, he pulled Genevieve up onto the platform with him.

"If I can have your attention please," he said in a raised voice. The room echoed with sounds of shushing as people tried to quieten each other. When the noise level was low enough he spoke triumphantly.

"Tonight, I am pleased to share with you my good fortune — Genevieve Simmons has agreed to be my wife." The whole room erupted with applause. Egged on by the crowd, Paul took Genevieve in his arms and kissed her on the mouth, much to the delight of the crowd.

For what seemed an age, Rebecca didn't move a muscle, staring at the entwined figures on the stage. He thought he had won; he thought they were playing a game, but he couldn't have been more wrong. Tia stood beside her friend, utterly mortified.

"This is getting way out of hand now. God knows if the two of them have been —" She couldn't finish the sentence. It made her feel sick to even imagine it.

Isabel looked at Rebecca, wishing she could have the love and admiration of a woman like her and hurting because she thought she never would. Genevieve's parents were on the stage affectionately patting Paul on the back as though he had just walked on water. He had done it, just like he said he would. Genevieve just stood there in the spotlight, unsure of what to do, but feeling like she had just made the biggest mistake of her life.

CHAPTER 19

THE NEXT MORNING, Genevieve was startled awake by her mother knocking on her bedroom door with great urgency.

"Come in," Genevieve groaned, pulling the cover from over her head. Her mother had a cup of tea in her hand, and her face was beaming.

"Good morning," she said brightly. "Did you sleep well?"

"Yes," Genevieve lied.

"Just to let you know, your father and I are over the moon about you and Paul. We really couldn't be happier for you." She sat down on the bed, oblivious to the turmoil Genevieve was experiencing at that moment.

Genevieve didn't know why she felt so unsettled, but it had something to do with her flatmate, Rebecca. There had been such intensity to their meeting yesterday, it was unnerving. She consciously pushed thoughts of Rebecca to the back of her mind and focused on what her mother was saying.

"So, we were thinking that the wedding should take place sooner rather than later. I mean, there's no need to procrastinate, is there?" her mother was rambling on. "If we start arranging it today we can set the date for a couple of months away." She didn't even wait for a response. "So I thought you and I could go wedding dress shopping today... and look what I have," she said secretively, withdrawing a credit card from her pocket. "Your father said the sky's the limit! Now come on, young lady." She stood up with the energy of a woman half her age. "Get your tea down you, get ready and let's go!"

After her mother left the room, Genevieve lay back down on the bed and wished she could share some of her mother's enthusiasm. Letting out a long sigh of resignation, she threw the quilt off her legs and sat at the edge of her bed. *It's going to be okay*, she thought. She pushed herself up off the bed, ignoring the steaming hot cup of tea her mother had left by her bedside, and decided she might as well get showered, get dressed and get the shopping trip over with.

Many hours and what seemed like a hundred dress changes later, Genevieve and her mother had finally settled on a plain silk wedding dress. Her mother was ecstatic but Genevieve was simply going through the motions — nothing felt real to her. She didn't know why she had agreed to marry Paul, why she had gone through with buying a wedding dress, and least of all, why she was now sitting at a restaurant table with her parents and Paul pretending that everything was alright when all she really wanted to do was scream out loud to expel the mounting sense of frustration she felt building within her.

She sat looking at them as though they were behind glass and she was unable to reach out and touch them.

"So, is anyone going to tell me about Rebecca then?" she asked suddenly. The question silenced them all and they looked at her sullenly. "What?" she asked, feeling defensive. "How am I ever going to get my memory back if you're keeping secrets from me? Can someone please tell me why there is such animosity between you all, or do I have to call her and ask her myself?"

It seemed to Genevieve that they looked as though they'd just been caught with their hands in the cookie jar.

"Isn't anyone going to speak?" she finally asked, losing her patience. Her parents looked hard at Paul, as if willing him to tell their daughter a plausible story to stop the questioning.

"Well," he said slowly, "it's a bit of a sore subject; that's why we haven't told you anything about it." Genevieve's mother looked anywhere but at her daughter, and her father took the wine bottle by the neck and poured himself a large glass.

"A sore subject for who?" she asked, her interest piqued.

"For me," he said, blushing slightly.

"Go on," she urged him.

"Well," he hesitated, glancing at her parents, then back to Genevieve, "it was after you had been living with her for a while." He began to build up momentum. "She basically ruined my chances of getting my own showcase by writing a very bad review about me."

"But why would she do that?" she asked incredulously. "You're a brilliant artist."

"Because," he looked at Eddie, who was shaking his head, "because... she was jealous of our relationship, Gen. We had words and things got a little out of hand, things were said that shouldn't have been said, and I was kinda blacklisted from the art world for a while. Things were quite tense between the two of you, and you weren't happy living there but you couldn't just move out because you owned half the place and your work studio was there." He smiled at her. "It doesn't matter now anyway, everything has turned out for the best."

Genevieve mulled over what he'd said.

"Why would she be jealous?"

He lowered his voice conspiratorially. "She's a lesbian, Gen. I was always under the impression she liked you. We didn't want to tell you because we didn't want to upset you. Will you forgive us?" he asked insincerely.

She could well imagine being angry at a critic who wrote a bad review for personal reasons rather than for the actual work at hand and she felt herself soften toward his explanation.

"Yes, of course," she said generously. "Well, you certainly showed her yesterday," she continued, squeezing his hand. He beamed.

"Yes I did, didn't I? I would appreciate it if you didn't mention this to anyone Gen; I think it's all best left in the past."

"Of course, I understand, Paul." The atmosphere around the table lightened almost immediately, and looks of relief flooded her parents' faces.

"I think today calls for a bottle of champagne to officially welcome our son into the family," Eddie said. He raised his hand to attract the waiter's attention.

"Yes, sir?" the young waiter asked.

"Your best bottle of champagne," Eddie said

benevolently, his eyes dancing. The waiter hurried off to the restaurant bar and arrived back a few moments later with a bottle of champagne, followed closely by another waiter carrying the champagne stand. He popped the cork and poured a taster for Eddie.

"That's fine." The waiter proceeded to fill the remaining glasses and left their table. "To Paul, the son I never had, and to Genevieve," he turned to look at her, tears welling in his eyes, "my darling daughter."

While her parents and Paul were sipping their drinks, Genevieve decided that if she was going to launch her bombshell, it had to be now or never.

"I have something to announce as well," she said smiling, though it didn't quite reach her eyes.

"What's that, darling?" Paul asked.

"Now I realise that there's understandably animosity between you and Rebecca, but I'd like to put that all behind us. As you said Paul, it is in the past. I've decided to move back to London," she said quickly. Eddie nearly sprayed his drink all over the table, whilst Elsie could only manage a gasp. Paul sat still, his face transfixed.

"Pardon?" he asked through gritted teeth. Genevieve took a deep breath.

"I'm moving back to London — at least until the wedding, anyway. Doctor Covette thinks it will be beneficial for me; she thinks I'm too far away from my real life and that a more familiar setting might help me to remember it." There was a stunned silence. Elsie closed her eyes and tried to control her breathing. Genevieve having her memory back was the last thing they wanted. *It's all going to be ruined, all of it,* she thought frantically.

"Did you not hear a word Paul said? She's a dirty lesbian! You can't go back there to have her warp your mind!" Eddie said in a sudden outburst of anger. Genevieve stared at her parents in surprise.

"So that's why neither of you like her — because she's a lesbian? Well don't worry about me; I have my own mind. It won't be warped by anyone," she said firmly. Elsie opened her eyes and looked at Eddie. His face was contorted with rage, and she could see he was fighting to control his temper. She put her hand under the table and squeezed his knee to get his attention, then pleaded with her eyes for him not to say any more. Genevieve nervously played with the napkin on her lap. They all looked at Paul, who had remained speechless. He finally managed to find his voice.

"So when did you decide this?" he asked quietly.

"Well, yesterday actually," she said anxiously, disconcerted by her father's reaction, "after my session with Doctor Covette. Look," she said, appealing to them all, "don't you see that even if I didn't like living there, there's a chance that going back to London could trigger some memories? I might be able to remember you all, and how much you must have meant to me." She smiled, attempting to give them reassurance. "Please, Mum, Dad, you don't have to worry about me. I'll be careful, I promise."

Paul's mind was racing. The only good side to this bombshell was that she had decided to go back **before** she saw Rebecca yesterday, so Rebecca could have had nothing to do with why she wanted to go home. He tried to work out whether there were any pros to her going back there but came up with none. If she returned to London and got her memory back, they were all doomed; him especially. The party mood definitely flattened and he found solace in the bottle with Eddie, who looked completely shaken up.

"Paul?" Genevieve said softly. He looked up from nursing his drink. "You said yourself that everything has worked out for the best with Rebecca. Can't you make up with her, for my sake?" she asked pleadingly. Paul shifted in his chair.

"I'd be willing to," he said, aware that he would have to change his battle plan, "but I don't know if she would bury the hatchet. If she doesn't, you living there could cause serious problems between us. She wouldn't allow me in your place before, so I don't think she'd let me in now."

"She seems like a reasonable person to me and I own half of it. I'll just have to talk to her, and if she cares about me as much as she seems to, she'll want to help me."

"Have you spoken to her about it?" Paul asked, looking down at the table.

"No, I wanted to tell you all first. I wasn't about to just pack my bags and run off in the middle of the night," she joked.

"When are you leaving then?" Eddie asked with fire in his eyes.

"I thought I'd give Rebecca a call this evening and see when it's the best time for me to move back. Speaking of which, Mum, you have her number, don't you?" Paul glanced at Elsie and knew she couldn't lie — after all, she'd texted Rebecca to ask her to send her things over.

"Yes love, I have it somewhere, I'll look for it later." A look of resignation crossed her face.

"Thanks, Mum," Genevieve beamed.

"Let's get the bill and get out of here," Eddie said gruffly.

* * *

Elsie and Genevieve were upstairs in the house, looking for Rebecca's number, while Paul and Eddie were sitting in the front room, whiskey on the table.

"I should have known this wouldn't work," Eddie said, getting up to pace the floor. Both men were in a state of panic.

"What's the next step then?" Paul asked quietly, aware of Eddie's frustration.

"There isn't anything we can do now, it's in God's hands," Eddie said.

"I'm sorry, Eddie. I feel as though I've let you and Elsie down," Paul said as he slumped down into a chair.

"It's not over yet son, she hasn't said she isn't going to marry you. She only said that she wants to go home to see if she can remember anything. Once the wedding is over, that will be the last any of us will have to do with that woman. Let's just hope Gen doesn't remember anything until then." Both of them simultaneously said a silent prayer.

Elsie knew exactly where Rebecca's number was, but made a big show of pretending to look for it. She felt that if she could delay the inevitable for a while longer, perhaps by some miracle Genevieve would change her mind. When she could put it off no longer, she pretended to have found it amongst her papers.

"Here it is!" she exclaimed, and handed the piece of paper over to her daughter with a heavy heart. She would have given her life to prevent her moving back to London, but she knew there was no stopping her once she had made her mind up. Genevieve took Elsie's hand, which both surprised and comforted her.

"Mum, please don't worry about me. You and Dad can come for dinner every Sunday. And you can take me to see all the sights, because I'm sure I won't remember where they are." Elsie knew she was only half-joking. She wrapped her daughter in a hug, the first real contact that she'd had with her in years. Tears rolled down her face. She had never cried in front of Genevieve before, but she couldn't control herself. She felt as if she was losing her daughter all over again, and with this new departure, a little piece of herself. Sensing her mother crying, Genevieve gently pulled back in order to face her.

"Please don't cry, Mum. If you don't want me to go straight away, I'll wait a few days. I suppose telling you so suddenly came as a bit of a shock, but you must have known I'd want to go home eventually." Even though Elsie could have told her that she'd prefer her to stay longer, there was no putting off the fact that Genevieve was going.

"No love, it's fine. I've just enjoyed having you here. Go and make the call." Elsie listened at the door whilst Genevieve called Rebecca — it was a very short call consisting of Rebecca confirming it was okay for Genevieve to move back in the following day. The next sound she heard was Genevieve beginning to gather her belongings together. She was grateful Genevieve could not hear the breaking of her heart.

CHAPTER 20

FILLED WITH TREMENDOUS anticipation, like a four-year-old waiting for Christmas, Rebecca stared at the telephone in her hand.

"Genevieve's coming home. She's coming home!" she said jubilantly to the empty space surrounding her. Unable to repress her excitement, she called Tia, who at first couldn't understand what Rebecca was saying because her voice was so high-pitched. When Tia finally made sense of the message, she too started to join in the excitement, telling Rebecca to get the drinks out because she'd be round within the hour. Tia hung up the phone and automatically called Isabel to tell her the news. She didn't have to be asked twice to go round to her apartment; her jacket was on before she'd even put the phone down.

The three women sat comfortably in Rebecca's apartment with only candles for light and music playing at a low volume in the background.

"What do you think brought this on?" Isabel asked. Rebecca couldn't erase her grin.

"I have absolutely no idea."

"Did she say anything about remembering?" Tia interjected.

"Nope, she just asked if she could come home tomorrow. That was it in a nutshell."

"Well, if she hasn't remembered anything, that

means she still has a fiancé," Tia remarked abruptly.

"I'm well aware of that," Rebecca said, her mood darkening. "The main thing is that I'll have her home. The other problems I'll deal with as-and-when. One thing I will not do is antagonise Paul, because that will lead her right into his hands."

"Becca?" Tia said.

"Yes," Rebecca replied testily.

"Um, not to put the dampers on anything, but what are you going to do when Paul decides he wants to stay over — in her bed?" Rebecca flinched at the thought.

"I don't know, I really don't know."

"Look, for all you know she might not be having any kind of relations with Paul, so until something is confirmed one way or another I wouldn't even go down that road," said Isabel. "This is really good news that she's coming back, Rebecca. There's a good chance that you can start opening her mind by showing her who she really is. Not about being a lesbian; but simply all the things you used to enjoy doing together. If anything, that way may prove more fruitful." Rebecca felt her spirits rising, buoyed on by Isabel's positive take on the situation.

"You're right."

"And just think, you'll be having her parents on your home turf now. No more of this macho bullshit," Tia said. "Do you want me to be here when she arrives tomorrow?"

"If you want to, but I don't want you annoying anyone."

"Me?" Tia said, pretending to look hurt.

"Yes, you!" she said, and turned to Isabel. "Do

you think it would be advisable to take Genie back to the crime scene?"

"I think you'd better play that one by ear; it could make things worse. I think you should just treat her as you would normally — without the physical contact, obviously."

"At least you won't be living in this big flat by yourself any more. So that just leaves me and you as singletons, Isabel," Tia said flirtatiously. Rebecca saw Isabel look away but the room wasn't dark enough to hide the fact that she was blushing.

* * *

Morning could not have come any sooner for Rebecca. The birds were singing, and she felt like joining them. She was once again grateful to Isabel, who had insisted that they all have an early night in order to not to wake up with a hangover. Rebecca had only consumed two glasses of wine, so she felt totally fresh and energised when she woke. She showered, taking time to enjoy the sensations of the massage setting. She ate a leisurely European breakfast of croissants, freshly squeezed orange juice and fresh fruit. She put on her jeans and the black V-neck top that Genevieve had said was her favourite, opting for sandals rather than boots as the sun was out and it had been forecast to be a hot day. She waited impatiently, and when she heard the bell she ran to the front door to answer the intercom.

"Hi, it's Genevieve." Those three simple words suddenly made her world a whole lot better. Rebecca buzzed her in and waited. She heard male voices coming down the hallway and was disappointed to think that Genevieve's parents had come with her, but to her relief, she opened the door to find two burly removal men.

"Where d'ya want them love?" one of them asked.

"Just here in the hallway would be great, thanks," said Rebecca. As she spoke, Genevieve appeared behind him. Rebecca was at a loss for words. Standing there, in the flesh, was Genevieve. She thought that this was perhaps how people felt when they were lost in the desert and saw a mirage. Thankfully though, this was no mirage; Genevieve was real — and to her delight they hugged one another.

"Welcome home," Rebecca said, releasing her. Genevieve's eyes widened in amazement as she took in the apartment.

"Wow, nice place."

"Well, you're to thank for the décor. It was you that put this place together." The removal man asked for a signature on his form, bade them a good day and left. Rebecca took Genevieve by her arm and led her into the front room. "Don't be a stranger in your own home," she said to her warmly.

"Oh, my god!" Genevieve said, amazed by the views the apartment afforded.

"Shall I show you around so you can familiarise yourself with everything?"

"Sure." Rebecca led her around the apartment, stopping when they got to the guest bedroom.

"This is your room," she said, looking intently at her features, searching for clues that would tell her whether Genevieve realised that she had not slept in there — not even once. When they had argued they had made it a number one rule: never to take fights into the bedroom. But there was no sign to show she remembered.

Shaking off the disappointment, Rebecca led her to her work studio. Again there was no recognition. *Take it slowly*, Rebecca reminded herself.

"Well, I'll leave you to get settled in. Do you need any help moving your things into your room?"

"No, but thank you, Rebecca," Genevieve said.

"If you need anything, just give us a yell." She left and walked thoughtfully back to the front room. Genevieve stood in her bedroom and for the second time in a few weeks was left wondering what sort of person had inhabited these walls. She went around the room, touching things, trying to get a feel of something — but there was nothing. She went back to the passage and brought all her things into the bedroom.

As she began unpacking them, her mind wandered back to the conversation she'd had with Paul the previous evening. Had Rebecca really been so mean? Would she really stop Paul from coming to the flat? She decided it was best to simply speak to Rebecca about it, and went in search of her in the front room. When she couldn't find her there, she looked for her bedroom. She peered in several open doors before she resorted to calling out for her. She followed the voice to the bedroom and knocked before entering.

The instant she pushed open the door, a flash of memory lasting no more than two or three seconds came back to her. Something very familiar... but she couldn't place what it was. She steadied herself by holding onto the door. Rebecca was by her side in an instant, and put her arm around her waist to walk her carefully to the bed.

"What happened?" she asked with concern in her voice.

"I had some sort of flashback — it happened so quickly, I don't know what it was about."

"Wait there while I get you some water," Rebecca said, and quickly went to the kitchen to get a bottle of water. When she came back to the bedroom, Genevieve looked pale.

"Are you feeling alright?" Rebecca asked. "Should I call a doctor?"

"No, I'm sorry to give you a fright. I'll be alright in a minute." She took a sip of water and let out a small sigh. "It's just been a stressful day today. My mum and dad were really upset that I was leaving. I think they're afraid something is going to happen to me again."

"How about I make us some lunch?"

"That would be great. Actually, I haven't eaten since this morning," Genevieve said, totally forgetting why she had gone in search of Rebecca in the first place.

"That'll be why you're looking so pale; you could never last long without refuelling yourself!"

While Rebecca prepared a meal of scallops and salad, the women discussed Genevieve's plans.

"I was hoping you could fill me in on my workload. I mean, was I working on anything before the accident happened?" Genevieve asked as she cut some fresh pesto bread into slices.

"You had just finished a large commission before the —" Rebecca stopped herself from using the word "attack". If Genevieve wanted to think of it as an accident, she would follow suit. "— accident. That morning, you were on your way to meet Ricardo Rawlings. He wanted you to provide him with a bespoke set of prints for his gallery, but you never made the appointment." She took two plates out of the cupboard and laid them on the worktop, then evenly divided the piping hot food onto each plate and added a side salad. She handed a plate to Genevieve.

"If it looks as good as it smells, I'm in for a treat." Genevieve inhaled deeply.

"This was one of your favourite dishes," Rebecca said, forking a piece of scallop into her mouth.

"So, do you think this Ricardo will still want me for the job?" Rebecca looked at her with a give-me-a-break expression.

"You're kidding, aren't you? He was trying to get you to work for him for months, but you were always too busy. The day you were going to meet him was your first free slot in ages. I think he would be delighted if you called him!"

"Oh good, 'cause I could really do with getting back to work," Genevieve said. "Sitting around twiddling my thumbs is not my idea of heaven."

"How about I get you his number and you call him after lunch? If you want, I can get Peter to run you over to see him. Peter would love to see you again." Genevieve gave Rebecca a quizzical look.

"Oh, Peter was — is — a friend of ours. He also doubles as my driver."

"You have a driver?" Genevieve asked in shock. Rebecca laughed.

"Yes, but only because I can't drive and my work takes me to different parts of London and often involves late nights, so it just makes sense."

"I see. I hope you don't mind me asking but the size of this apartment has made me think... Do I earn a lot of money? I didn't even think to ask my parents about my finances."

"A fair amount. Don't worry about it; you have everything you need to know filed away in the cabinet in your studio. All the bills for this place come out of our joint account."

"We have a joint account? she asked, almost absently."

"Yes, our lives were tied together in a lot of ways." Rebecca replied with inexplicable sadness.

"This food is good," Genevieve said, quickly changing the subject. She didn't understand the meaning behind some of the things Rebecca said, and it made her feel uncomfortable. Not in a bad way, but in a way that reinforced how little she knew of herself and how reliant she was on strangers to build a picture of who she was. They ate the remainder of their lunch in silence. Once they'd finished, Rebecca loaded the dishwasher and went to retrieve Ricardo's number for Genevieve.

Watching Genevieve on the telephone to Ricardo, Rebecca admired the way she was handling things. She'd always known that Genevieve was a strong person; but to see her in action with the odds stacked against her, still moving forward, gave her a new admiration for her. Despite what had to be one of the most earth-shattering experiences one could come across, she had remained in control. Just sitting in their apartment was testament to that; Rebecca could only imagine what Genevieve had faced when she informed her parents that she was moving back to London — not only to live so far away, but also with a woman who they believed was the devil itself.

Genevieve put the phone down and smiled happily.

"Well, you were right, he seems very anxious for me to 'get to work straight away' as he put it," she said, mimicking his voice. They both laughed. "He asked me to drop round this evening. If it's okay, I'd like to take up the offer of that lift."

"I'll give Peter a call."

"There's something I wanted to talk to you about first — this animosity between you and Paul," Genevieve suddenly said awkwardly. Rebecca stiffened, not sure of how to respond. "He's agreed to bury the hatchet and I'd be really grateful if you do the same. I don't want any bad feeling when he comes round." She was looking intently at Rebecca, as if trying to gauge her reaction.

"Of course, I have no problem with Paul," Rebecca said with a tentative smile, wondering what story Paul had fed her.

When Peter arrived to pick Genevieve up at the front of the apartment block, Rebecca thought he was going to start crying. His face turned bright red as he tried to contain his emotions and his Adam's apple bobbed in his throat. He hugged Genevieve so tightly Rebecca thought he would break her ribs. Genevieve seemed to have become used to the over-familiarity of those who were strangers to her, and she was laughing happily as they set off in the car for her appointment. Once they had disappeared into the traffic, Rebecca went back upstairs to their apartment, where for the first time in months she fell into a deep sleep.

She awoke abruptly to the sounds of laughter and muffled conversation. It was dark outside and a cover was laying over her. She sat up, pushed her fingers through her hair and got out of bed. In her en-suite bathroom, she turned on the cold water tap and splashed her face with water. She heard footsteps outside her room. They went into the bathroom, then after a few moments the toilet flushed and the footsteps retraced themselves back to the front room. Her stomach turned. Without going out there, she knew it was Paul. She sat on the toilet seat with her head in her hands. She was at a loss for what to do and felt like a stranger in her own home. She went back into the bedroom and picked up the phone, her hands shaking. She dialled the number.

"Please answer." Relief flooded her body when Tia answered her phone. "I need you now. More than ever," she said desperately. Tia arrived at her apartment door within ten minutes. She'd been about to attend a work do in Soho when she received Rebecca's call. She'd caught a taxi straight away and now she was standing outside her front door, fuming that Paul was going to play this out to the last. Rebecca opened the door and led her quickly into her bedroom, closing the door quietly behind her.

"Why are we hiding in here?" she demanded. "This is your place."

"Wait, we need to talk about this," Rebecca said with a glazed look of hopelessness in her eyes.

"There's nothing to talk about. He needs to leave, and now!" She was raising her voice. "Shh," Rebecca pleaded, "they'll hear you." She glanced cautiously towards the door.

"So what! Becca, what is wrong with you? Why are you letting him get away with this shit?" Tia was seething with frustration.

"I don't want to scare Genie away, Tia. If I go in there guns blazing, telling him to leave, what reason am I supposed to give? She's already asked me to bury the hatchet with him."

"That's an easy one: You're her lover. He's not. And for good measure, tell her that her parents are mental! That sounds about right to me. I can't understand how you've put up with pussy-footing around these people for so long. Bloody tell her that if she doesn't like it — tough! She's not a china doll, Becca. She won't break if you say the word 'lesbian' to her. Jesus Christ." She sat on the bed. There was a soft knock at the door.

"Rebecca?" Genevieve called gently. Rebecca looked at Tia and didn't reply. She put her finger to her lips.

"Fuck this," said Tia and stood up. Before Rebecca had a chance to stop her, she had opened the door.

"Genevieve," she said brightly.

"Oh, hi Tia, I didn't know you were here." Genevieve embraced her.

"I haven't been here long." Genevieve peeked over Tia's shoulder.

"Is Rebecca alright?"

"Yes, she's fine, she's just woken up."

"We're going to get an Indian takeaway. I just wondered if you wanted anything?" Before Rebecca could reply, Tia said, "Come to think of it, we haven't had an Indian in a while, have we Becca? We'd love some. In fact, since it's a Friday I think I'll give Isabel a call and see if she'd like to join us as well."

"Okay," Genevieve said, completely unfazed by Tia's gate-crashing.

"Excellent. Okay, we'll be out in a minute, and then we can order." Genevieve turned to leave, and Tia shut the door.

"Are you mad?" Rebecca said.

"No, I'm majorly pissed off. This has got to stop, because not only is it going to make you ill, it's going to make me ill as well! When did you become so repressed?" Rebecca ignored Tia's question.

"I'll call Isabel, shall I?" she said, and added sarcastically, "Anybody else?"

"Now you mention it, yes. Do you know that since you've been using work as an excuse not to see anyone, you have locked out your friends who genuinely care about you and want to help you get through this?" said Tia.

"Tia, this is the only way I can deal with this at the moment. I don't want to be crowded by people asking me questions I don't have the answers to. This is hard enough, please, don't make it any harder." Rebecca got up from the bed and grabbed her mobile phone from the dressing table.

"Okay, keep the shutters down, but I don't want to see you behaving like a bloody wimp anymore," said Tia, relenting. "Now, get that gorgeous woman over here." There was a wry smile in her eyes. Rebecca called Isabel, who said she'd like nothing better than to join them. Then they made their way into the front room, but were stopped in their tracks at the entrance. Sitting on the sofa opposite Genevieve and Paul were Genevieve's parents. Tia nearly burst out laughing.

"Sorry it's a full house," Genevieve said, "but I forgot some things at my parents' house and they decided to drop them off."

Rebecca managed to find her voice and croaked, "No problem at all, the more the merrier." She tried to step backwards, but Tia blocked her way and pushed her forward into the room. "Can I get anyone a drink?" Rebecca asked hospitably, moving swiftly into the kitchen.

"It's okay, I've just refilled everyone's glass," Genevieve called after her. Rebecca poured a glass of wine for herself and Tia, but nearly dropped them both on the floor when she returned to the front room and saw Tia seated between Paul and Genevieve, faking oblivion to the dagger stares of her parents. *This girl is going to be the death of me*, she thought. She set the wine glasses down on the table and sat in a vacant armchair by the window.

"So how are you finding London on your first day back?" Tia asked, breaking the silence.

"Fine," Genevieve answered. "I'm amazed at the view from this apartment."

"Oh yes, you've spent many a time happily gazing through that window. You were going to paint the view, but you never got round to it, what with your busy schedule." Rebecca took a nervous sip of her wine.

"I'll definitely get round to it now," she said firmly. The room lapsed into silence again and when the doorbell buzzed Rebecca jumped up to answer it. She opened the door and, straight away, warned Isabel under her breath, "Her parents are in there."

Isabel's eyes widened, and she mouthed back, "You're joking?" Rebecca shook her head as she let her in.

"Where's Tia?" Isabel whispered.

"Doing what she does best — winding them up," Rebecca said curtly.

"Oh, goody." A crafty smile crossed Isabel's lips. When they walked back into the front room, Paul and Eddie could not disguise their discomfort.

"Is this an official visit?" Eddie asked.

"No, a social one in fact," Isabel replied confidently.

"Is that allowed then?" Eddie asked with a touch of irritation.

"Well, as long as I'm not mixing with any offenders in here, I think it's alright," Isabel replied sarcastically.

"Can I get you a drink?" Rebecca asked.

"A glass of wine would be great, thanks." Rebecca disappeared into the kitchen and Isabel sat in her chair. She acknowledged Tia, then turned her attention to Genevieve.

"Are you settling in okay?"

"Yes, as a matter of fact, I wanted to tell everyone I had some memory flashbacks today." She looked expectantly at Paul and her parents.

"Did you?" Isabel said slowly, surveying the room. The atmosphere had immediately changed from hostile to fearful.

"Yes, but it happened so quickly I don't know what it was about." Relief flooded her parents' and Paul's faces. "That's a good sign though, isn't it?" she said, directing the question to her parents, who nodded mutely.

"Hopefully you'll get your memory back in no time, and you can put this horridness behind you and carry on life as it was before," Isabel said innocently.

"Genevieve," Elsie said changing the subject, "I'm keeping your wedding dress at the house seeing as you're leaving from there. It just makes sense to get ready from home."

"Yes, Mum."

"I can't wait," Paul said, and looked past Tia to wink at Genevieve.

"Oh, I love weddings! Do tell about the dress. Is it white?" Tia smiled wryly at Elsie.

"Yes, it's white," Elsie said, playing along with her sarcasm. The women's gazes locked as though they were boxers in a ring, weighing up their opponents. Tia felt like screaming. She was aware that Genevieve had lost her memory, but had she lost her mind as well? Could she not feel the "something's not quite right" atmosphere in the room? Had the blow to her head dulled her senses as well?

"Shall I order the food then?" Genevieve asked, standing up.

"Yes, please do," Tia said. Then she mumbled under her breath, "This is going to be fun."

After forty-five minutes of awkward conversation, Genevieve called from the kitchen,

"The table is set!" The Indian meal had been delivered five minutes earlier, and she'd already emptied the contents into bowls for self-serving. The three women sat at one end of the large glass table while Paul, Genevieve and her parents sat at the other end. The talk at the table was terse. Tia tried to make light of the situation by telling Genevieve anecdotes about her past life, like the time Tia had persuaded Genevieve, as a joke, that the copy of a masterpiece she had was the real McCoy; the painting had actually managed to fool some well-to-do people in the art world as well. The women laughed like they were teenagers again. Genevieve's parents' and Paul's faces, however, remained sombre throughout and they made small talk amongst themselves instead.

After dinner, the three women remained at the table and became ever more intoxicated while Genevieve reluctantly joined her parents and Paul in the front room. They left shortly after, and Genevieve told the women she was going to bed. Despite their pleas for her to join them, she declined and went to her room, where she lay listening to the hysterical laughter that drifted into her bedroom as the woman recounted disastrous dates they had been on. For some reason, Genevieve found herself trying desperately to listen for Rebecca's voice.

CHAPTER 21

GENEVIEVE WOKE UP early, despite not getting to sleep until very late. She looked around her bedroom, trying to see if anything seemed familiar — the blinds, the rug, the art — but to no avail; her memory still eluded her. She had so many things on her mind. She'd heard the front door close the night before and assumed that all the guests had left but when she'd walked into the front room she'd seen Rebecca and Isabel seated together on the sofa with candles burning, looking very cosy together. After she returned to her bed it had dawned on her that perhaps Rebecca and Isabel were lovers. She didn't know if what she was feeling was shock, but she certainly felt it intensely.

She began to wonder if Rebecca's sexuality was the only reason her parents didn't like Rebecca, and whether Paul's excuse was even true. Her father's outburst at the restaurant had certainly made it seem that way. Homosexuality was her parents' number one hate, as she'd discovered a few days previously while watching a news report on gay civil services. The torrent of abuse her father had yelled at the TV had shocked her. She didn't know if this was normal behaviour for him, but it was very intense. Her mother had quickly changed the channel and he had calmed down. She didn't know what her own attitude to homosexuality had been, but she couldn't imagine being homophobic if she was living with a lesbian.

She still couldn't understand why her parents

hadn't just told her, or more importantly, why Paul hadn't told her. He wasn't a bigot as far as she knew, and wasn't one to mince words either. She wondered if Rebecca had been seeing Isabel for a long time or if they'd been thrown together by her accident. *What about Tia — is she one too? Does she only have female friends, or does she have male ones too?*

She heard Rebecca moving about outside her room and suddenly felt too embarrassed to face her. *What if Isabel is still there?* It would be awkward — maybe moving back in without actually knowing what was what had been a bad idea. She called Paul on her mobile and arranged to meet him for lunch on Shaftsbury Avenue.

She was having a long leisurely bath in her en-suite bathroom when she heard Rebecca knocking at her bedroom door. Her first reaction was to cover her body, but then she felt silly. She didn't think Rebecca was the type of person who would just invade some one's privacy.

"Are you okay?" Rebecca called through the door.

"Yes, thanks," she called back.

"I'm off to work now, I'll see you later." When she heard the front door close, she let out a long sigh of relief. She was being paranoid, she reprimanded herself. So what if she was living with a lesbian — she wasn't going to try anything on her. *Anyway*, she thought, *she knows I'm straight because I'm getting married* — and with that she slid right down into the bath, letting the water cover her face.

* * *

The small size of the French restaurant Genevieve had chosen only added to its charm. Paul ordered them a glass of Chianti each and they waited for the waiter to leave before speaking.

"You sounded upset on the phone," he said.

"Yes, I was... am." She took a sip of her wine, letting the sourness dissolve on her taste buds. Then she looked him straight in the eye, daring him to lie. "I don't like the truth being withheld from me." He shifted uncomfortably on his chair, examining the glass in his hand distractedly.

"I don't know what you're talking about." He pulled the front of his t-shirt away from the base of his neck.

"Rebecca," she said accusingly.

He blinked rapidly. "What about her?"

"That was all rubbish about her writing a bad review, wasn't it?" He stared at her, reading her face.

"Don't be silly."

"That's it." She stood up to leave, and when he grabbed her by the arm, she shook it off. "If you can sit there and lie to me about this, then what else have you been lying to me about? How can I trust you?" He stood up, defeated.

"Okay, sit down — please... How did you find out?"

"I just know, Paul. She's nothing like you portrayed her. And if you don't tell me the truth now, I'll just ask her myself."

"Okay, okay. Look, your parents don't like her for obvious reasons. I wanted to tell you the truth, but your parents thought it was best if you didn't know. They think she's a bad influence on you. I tried to tell them that you would find out eventually anyway, but they weren't having it. You know how stubborn your dad is Gen, so I just went along with it. They've never liked you living with her and they thought they'd be able to keep you at their house." He looked down at the table as Genevieve glared at him, not knowing whether to believe his latest story.

"Is there anything else either you or my parents are withholding from me?" she said, dismayed by his revelations.

"Of course not, Gen." He looked directly into her eyes.

"Why couldn't you have just been honest with me from the start, Paul? It would have been so much easier. I felt trapped in that house. I wouldn't be surprised to hear that they'd even stopped my friends from contacting me."

"Don't be too hard on them, Gen. I'm sorry, we were just doing what we thought was best for you... I promise you, no more secrets from now on."

"Okay," she said, still brooding.

"Have you told Rebecca that you know she's a lesbian?" Paul asked flatly.

"No."

"I wouldn't let on to her that you know. You don't want her to think we've been talking about her."

"Do you think so?"

"Yes, I do." He changed the subject abruptly. "Anyway, enough about other people and their love lives, have you and your mum drawn up a list of people we're going to invite?"

"I haven't, but I'm sure mum has. Going as far back as when I was a baby, no doubt!"

"Have you thought about bridesmaids?"

"No," she said, not wanting to talk about it.

"I'm sorry, I shouldn't be putting pressure on you. I'm beginning to sound like your mum." He took her hand in his but she pulled away.

"Paul, to be honest with you, I'd rather just elope. I don't want to be at my own wedding and not know anyone." She caught her breath for a moment as another memory flashed into her mind. She felt herself getting frustrated — that was the second time that it had happened, and both times they had made no sense. Paul assumed that her tense body language was from their earlier argument.

"You know me," he said again, taking her hand in his.

Do I, Paul? Do I really know you?

* * *

Genevieve returned home before Rebecca and decided to order a gourmet meal for them both from one of the menus Tia had told her about when she'd spoken to her earlier. It was delivered already prepared, and all she had to do was put it in the oven for the right amount of time. She hoped tonight would be an opportunity to get everything out into the open, despite Paul telling her not to say anything; she was tired of people ordering her about.

She felt grimy after being in central London all day so she quickly showered and changed her clothes. Afterwards, she set the table for two, changing it several times because it looked too intimate with candles and flowers. In the end, she decided she didn't care if it looked intimate; it was stunning and that's all she cared about. She didn't hear Rebecca come in until Rebecca was standing right behind her.

"Expecting company?" she asked. Genevieve jumped.

"Oh, you scared me."

"I'm sorry."

"Who's the lucky guest?" Rebecca asked again, nodding toward the table.

"You are."

"Me?" She was taken aback. Had Genevieve remembered?

"Yes, you. And before you get worried, I ordered ready-made meals."

"So you found your bag of dinner party tricks, did you?" Rebecca laughed. Genevieve may have been a great artist, but a good cook she wasn't. She had collected an array of freshly cooked menus, which she used to pass off as her own cooking. At the end of many a dinner party, all of the guests were in on the joke that she hadn't prepared the food herself.

"Yes, Tia called for you earlier; she said she couldn't reach you on your mobile, and I told her I was cooking for you. Well, it took her more than a few minutes to stop laughing and tell me where to find my menus."

"Thank God for Tia is all I can say! No offence, but..."

"I can imagine," Genevieve said good-naturedly.

"Smells delicious, have I got time to clean up?"

"Yep, can I pour you a glass of chilled wine?"

"You certainly can," Rebecca said, walking to

her bedroom. Once inside the sanctuary of her room, she leaned against the door, head tilted towards the ceiling. When she had first walked in, for a few seconds she had imagined that everything had gone back to how it was before. But then she had looked into Genevieve's eyes and seen the vagueness there, and she was brought back to reality with a thump.

It had been crushing not being able to just walk up and hold Genevieve, not to have any physical contact. She stripped off her clothes, showered and put her jeans and T-shirt on before returning to the kitchen where Genevieve was making a lot of noise but not actually doing very much.

"Would you like a hand?" she asked, seeing her flustered.

"I think I may need more than a hand," Genevieve said, trying to take the food out of the oven when it clearly wasn't ready.

"Why don't you sit down and let me finish up?" Rebecca said.

"But I wanted to make you a nice meal!" Genevieve protested.

"And you have done, the table looks amazing. Honestly, it's fine, this cooker needs some getting used to." Genevieve sat down while Rebecca confidently got things under control in the kitchen.

"So what did you do today?" Rebecca asked, her back to her.

"Met Paul for lunch."

"Oh, anywhere nice?"

"A little French place on Shaftsbury Avenue." Rebecca stopped momentarily as she fought to keep her emotions calm. That was their favourite haunt.

They went there most Sundays. Was it just a coincidence?

"Who recommended it?"

"No one, we were passing, and I liked the look of it. And believe it or not, I had another flashback today." Rebecca spun round excitedly, but upon seeing Genevieve's face, she knew it had been nothing significant.

"Just another quick flash, I'm afraid." Rebecca finished up in the kitchen and served the food. They sat enjoying it for a few moments.

"How long have you been friends with Isabel?" Genevieve asked. Her face remained focused on her plate.

"Only a short while, ever since your accident or around about that time. Why do you ask?"

"No particular reason." Genevieve kept her eyes on her food.

"Genie, don't forget at this moment in time I know you better than you know yourself. And I know when there is a question behind a question, so out with it."

"It's nothing, honestly, I was just thinking it's a bit strange you having a police officer as your friend, considering your work background. And before you ask me if I'm being elitist, no, I'm not — it just seems a weird combination."

"We have a lot more in common than our careers."

"Like what?" Genevieve asked innocently.

"Just things," Rebecca said, taking a last mouthful of food.

"Now look who's being evasive."

"I'm not being evasive; I'm just saying there are more to people sometimes than their jobs."

"Have it your way." Genevieve stood up abruptly and took her empty plate to the kitchen. Rebecca, bemused by her reaction, called out after her,

"Am I missing something here?"

Genevieve reappeared and looking intensely at Rebecca, said, "Are you —" The doorbell buzzed. Rebecca looked at Genevieve,

"Are you expecting someone?" She shook her head.

"Neither am I, shall we ignore it?"

"What if it's important?"

"It had better be." Rebecca got up from the table and threw her napkin down. "You can ask me that question in a minute."

She pressed the intercom to be informed that Paul was downstairs, and though she was annoyed, she buzzed him up. She walked back to the table. "Paul is here to see you." She saw the irritation on Genevieve's face.

"I only saw him a few hours ago," she said, clearing the condiments from the table.

"We'll have to have that talk some other time. Thanks for dinner, I think I'll go to my room and read." Rebecca quickly walked to her room and closed the door. She wasn't sure what Genevieve knew, but she didn't want to go down the route of discussing her sexuality. Not yet anyway.

Genevieve could have killed Paul — he had the most annoying habit of turning up when she least expected him. He came bounding into the room, happiness written all over his face, a bottle of champagne in one hand and a large bouquet of flowers in the other.

"Guess what?" Her irritation was momentarily lost.

"What?" she said with a flash of curiosity.

"Who's just sold a shitload of his paintings for top dollar?" He put the champagne and flowers on the table and swept Genevieve up in his arms, twirling her around as though she were a rag doll.

"You did?" she said, laughing. "Paul, I'm so happy for you."

"Two glasses, please," he said, lowering her back to the floor. She went into the kitchen cupboard and took out two champagne flutes and placed them on the table while he popped open the champagne. Meanwhile, she put the bouquet of roses in a vase.

"Here's to the future." Paul lifted his glass into the air, his face shining with pride.

"To the future." They clinked glasses and drank their champagne. They stayed up late into the evening, drinking and talking. Genevieve's earlier anger toward him softened with the alcohol. She got up to pour another drink but Paul grabbed her hand and playfully pulled her back down into his arms.

"Do you know what would make me the happiest man alive tonight?" he asked her, his eyes saying it all.

Rebecca's nightmare was coming true. She hadn't been able to do anything but listen to their muffled conversation all evening, and now she heard Paul and Genevieve make their way into her room, giggling together, obviously intoxicated. She didn't know whether to go in there and put a stop to it or just think logically and try to ignore it, but she couldn't do either. She was feeling real, physical pain and the tears were streaming down her face. She grabbed hold of her pillow and hugged it while she rocked herself. She didn't know if their relationship could make it back from here — even if Genevieve recovered her memory. She didn't think she would ever forget this moment. She pushed her head down into her pillow and screamed months of pain into the enveloping softness. When she could no longer stand it she jumped out of bed, put on her jogging clothes, and ran out of the flat.

She darted over to the embankment and sank to her knees, sobbing. She felt a vibration in her pocket. She took out her mobile phone in case it was Genevieve, but the caller ID showed it was Isabel. She flipped open the phone and could barely speak a word of English. Gibberish noises came out of her mouth. Isabel was talking loudly in the ear piece. Her voice sounded alarmed but not panicked.

"Rebecca, tell me where you are," she kept repeating. Rebecca must have told her, because the next thing she knew she was being embraced by Isabel.

"That fucking bastard, that fucking bastard," Rebecca kept repeating. Isabel managed to piece together what had happened. She was someone who normally knew how to fix everything, but this was irreparable. Rebecca eventually calmed down a little and hugged her friend tightly.

"I'm sorry you have to keep seeing me like this."

"I wouldn't have it any other way," Isabel joked. "Though I may start charging you for my dry cleaning bill. Maybe I should go back to the apartment and kick the shit out of him myself. He's seriously in need of help, to have pulled a stunt like this! The man is obviously a psychopath. Do you want to come and stay at my place tonight?" Rebecca nodded, and Isabel helped her up as though she were a fragile old woman, walking her gently to her car.

* * *

The effects of the champagne and the wine Genevieve had drunk made her head feel giddy. She was in the bathroom brushing her teeth when she heard the front door close. *Probably Rebecca going to meet Isabel*, she thought, a stab of jealousy shooting through her. Was she going insane? Why should she feel so jealous...? She turned off the bathroom light and walked back into her bedroom where Paul was already in bed, sitting up, his bare chest exposed. She saw his underwear and jeans on the floor, and the realisation hit her that he was naked. She froze as she realized that she felt absolutely no rush of desire or any urgency to join him. Feeling a mixture of fear and apprehension instead, she thought of a way to stall him. If she gave him more alcohol, maybe he would drop off to sleep, but seeing how alert he was, she doubted it. She wished Rebecca was in the other room — maybe then she could have used the excuse of needing to talk to her and escaped this situation.

She got into bed fully dressed in her pyjamas. She stretched to turn off the bedside lamp, but he stopped her.

"No, I want to see you." He drew her close to him and she could feel that he already had an erection. A sudden feeling of repulsion came over her, and she tried to wriggle away from it, but it only caused him to hold her tighter. He covered her mouth with his, his tongue forcing her lips apart. She started to panic. She felt as though she were being suffocated — it was all so wrong.

Suddenly, he seemed to change right before her eyes. His hair looked softer, his facial features more feminine, his shoulders were slender. And then as quickly as his appearance had changed, it reverted back again. She gave one large heave and pushed him off her.

"What's the matter?" he asked with an alarming flash of cold anger.

"It's you, you look different," she said, scrambling off the bed. "Look Paul, I think it's best if you leave. I can't do this." Her voice was shaking. He looked enraged, and fear took hold of her again. She backed away into the bathroom.

"What the fuck is wrong with you?" he yelled, his face fiercely distorted. He lunged off the bed toward the bathroom but he wasn't fast enough and she managed to slam the door and lock it.

"I want you to leave now!" she shouted, "Rebecca will be back soon." Paul banged on the bathroom door like a man possessed.

"I don't care who is coming back, I won't let you do this to me again, do you hear me?" Genevieve cowered on the floor next to the toilet, unable to comprehend the change in him. After a few minutes, the banging stopped and she heard him moving about. Presumably he was gathering his clothes together. After what seemed a lifetime, the bedroom door closed. She waited until she heard the front door slam before she went out to make sure he had really left.

She double-bolted the door and put the safety chain on, then went through to the kitchen to pour herself a neat whiskey. Shaken, she switched the side lights on in the front room and lay on the sofa, drinking steadily, trying to get rid of the nagging questions. *Why had Paul morphed into a female figure? Was there something wrong with her? Were her parents right? Was Rebecca's lifestyle warping her mind?* The thought of Rebecca sent shivers down her spine. *I wonder what she's doing now*, she thought enviously. The image of Rebecca lying naked in bed with another woman made her feel unsettled. She asked herself over and over again why she was feeling like this. She was straight — she didn't feel that way towards women! But why had Paul said that he wouldn't let her do this to him **again**? What exactly had she done?

She finished the rest of the whiskey in one gulp and poured herself another one. Genevieve stared around the room as if seeing it for the first time. Her gaze fell on the portrait of Rebecca, the overhead lamp highlighting her beautiful face, relaxed and serene. She found herself staring at it intently. The alcohol seemed to be lubricating her mind. The more she looked at the painting, the more it seemed to be stirring her memory.

With some effort, she heaved herself off the sofa, feeling more drunk than she'd realised. Putting her empty glass on the coffee table she walked unsteadily to the painting. Leaning closer to it she whispered, "What is it about you?" Her voice had the ever-so-faint slur of too much alcohol. She traced the outline of Rebecca's profile with her finger, stopping when she reached her throat. She could feel a slight memory of painting the portrait; something was etched at the back of her mind. She squeezed her eyes tightly shut, as if she could force the memory out into the open.

Suddenly, without warning, she felt as though her soul had been unchained and the realisation descended slowly into her mind. She stared wide-eyed at the chain around Rebecca's neck. The numbers 143 meant something — she was sure of it. She felt a deep sense of bewilderment as she tried to make sense of it. She hadn't seen Rebecca wearing that chain, so why was it so familiar to her? A memory began to tremble on the horizon of her mind. All of a sudden, like a bolt from the blue, it came to her. The jealousy, the feelings of disloyalty when she was with Paul, nothing else could explain it — she had felt like that because she was in love with Rebecca. 143 stood for "I love you."

Amid the stillness of the night, memories began to filter through her mind, slowly at first. Rebecca finding it difficult to sit still whilst she sketched her; Genevieve laughing and promising to make it worth her while; their lovemaking afterwards... and finally, giving Rebecca the finished painting and Rebecca saying in confusion, "I don't have a chain like that."

Then the realisation dawning — the embedded message — and the look in Rebecca's eyes that spoke of her love for Genevieve.

Suddenly, the prison that had been holding her memories captive sprang open, setting them free. She fell down on a chair, startled as though she had been struck, her mind reeling.

"What the fuck!" she said aloud. Everything about her life came back to her in what seemed like a second — everything except the day of the attack, which was of secondary importance at that moment.

She poured herself another drink, her hands shaking, anger rising. She had nearly slept with Paul, and Rebecca had left the apartment probably to be with Isabel. A sense of personal violation spread throughout her at the thought of what Rebecca, Paul and her family had done to her.

* * *

The next morning, Isabel reluctantly dropped Rebecca back at her apartment. Rebecca insisted she wanted to go back alone. If this was the way it was going to be, she would have to learn to deal with it. There was no way of wrapping herself up in cotton wool, and even if there was, she wouldn't stand for it. She stood at the kerb, watching Isabel drive away, preparing herself for the daunting prospect which lay ahead of her. Paul had won. He had Genevieve; there was nothing else to fight for. She would go and see Carla on Monday morning and arrange for their financial matters to be dealt with. She would see to it that Genevieve's business would not be hung out for the world to see.

She stood in the lift and reminisced about how her time had begun with Genevieve four years previously. *What goes around comes around*, she thought bitterly. She had no right to be angry with Paul. Had she not done exactly the same thing to him? She walked out of the lift, keys in hand, praying they weren't out of bed yet. She needed a little time to pull herself together. She put the key in the door and went to push it open, but it didn't budge.

"What the..." she stopped herself saying it out loud, and swore under her breath. Great, now she would have to wake them up, and she looked like shit. She rang the bell several times before she heard movements in the passage. She hoped it wasn't Paul, and was relieved when she heard Genevieve's voice. The door opened a crack.

"Rebecca?"

"Yes." Genevieve closed the door to release the safety chain. She looked worse than Rebecca felt. Her hair was a mess, her face was puffy and she stunk of alcohol.

"Are you okay?" Rebecca asked with an expression of concern across her face.

"What do you think?" she replied shuffling down the hall.

"Where's Paul?" Rebecca asked hurriedly following behind her.

"Not here, that's for sure," she said refusing to look at her.

"Did you two have an argument?" Rebecca grabbed hold of her and turned her around. Genevieve pulled her arm away and looked straight into her eyes.

"You could say that. Have you been with Isabel?" The bitterness was evident in her voice.

"Yes... What happened here?" Genevieve turned around and walked toward her bedroom.

"Nothing. Look, I really feel like crap. I need to sleep."

"Genie, did he hurt you?" Genevieve didn't answer, she just walked into her bedroom and slammed the door.

CHAPTER 22

GENEVIEVE AWOKE in the late afternoon, feeling an incessant stream of sunshine on her face. Her hangover was bad. She felt as if someone was busy hammering inside her head. Memories of the previous night assaulted her. The memories of Rebecca were coming back to her. The thought of Paul naked in her bed, touching her, then his anger when she fled; it aroused nothing but pity for him. She edged out the bed, mindful of her headache, which only seemed to get worse with movement, and slowly walked to the bathroom. She groaned when she saw her reflection in the mirror. Her eyes were swollen and red; she looked like a boxer who'd gone twelve rounds. She brushed her teeth and took a cold shower. Shivering, she dried herself, put on a white night shirt and made her way toward the kitchen.

As she walked into the front room, she was hit by blazing sun rays showering the room with golden warmth. Shielding her eyes with her hand, she walked around into the kitchen. She was startled to find Rebecca standing by the worktop, making tea.

"I didn't realise you were home, I thought you would have gone out," she said. She tried to appear normal as she rummaged through the kitchen drawer looking for the painkillers. Finding them, she poured herself a glass of water.

"Feeling rough?" Rebecca asked sympathetically, avoiding looking at her whilst she poured the boiling water into her tea cup.

"You could say that," she said.

"So what was that in aid of?" Rebecca said, stirring her tea, the metal of the spoon clinking against the porcelain cup. Genevieve looked at her, perplexed.

"The drinking binge, I mean. You don't normally knock it back like that."

"Oh, nothing really," Genevieve said as she drew a chair away from the table and slid onto it, popping the tablets into her mouth and chasing them with a swig of water. "Just things with Paul." She lowered her head, not wanting to meet Rebecca's eyes and reveal the anger there. "And you," she added.

"Me?" Rebecca's eyes widened at hearing this. "Have I done something to upset you?" Holding her tea, she sat down at the table opposite Genevieve.

"I don't know, Rebecca, you tell me. Have you done anything that could have upset me?" The anger was rising inside her once more.

"Nothing springs to mind," Rebecca said breezily, her eyes innocent and empty.

"Are you sleeping with Isabel?" Genevieve glared at her. Rebecca nearly choked on the tea that was making its way down her throat. She put the cup down unsteadily, spilling some over the edge. When she finally got herself together, she was aghast.

"No, no I'm not. What would make you think a thing like that?" She stood up to get some tissue and wiped the spilled tea off the table. Here Rebecca had been going through her own hell, thinking that Genevieve had slept with Paul the night before, and now this bombshell!

"Did you sleep with Paul last night?" Rebecca

asked her, sitting back down and wishing her tea was something stronger as she waited for the answer.

"And why would you care?" Genevieve answered sarcastically. "I mean, you certainly haven't seemed too concerned up until now about Paul and me." Her strong stare fixed itself on Rebecca's face. Rebecca looked confused.

"I don't understand what you're talking about."

"Oh, of course you don't, how could you?" Genevieve looked at her as if she was a total stranger. "Your girlfriend gets attacked and loses her memory, and the one person she should have been able to trust inexplicably lies to her. And not only that, she leaves me with a man who is trying to sleep with me, while she runs off in the middle of the night with another woman!"

Rebecca was rigid in her chair, her cheeks drained of colour.

"That's right, Becca," Genevieve said bitterly. "I remember."

"When?" She coughed; her throat was dry and she was finding it difficult to swallow.

"What difference does it make? I know," she said shaking her head sadly. "I would have believed just about anybody could have betrayed me... anybody else but you, Becca." Tears brimmed in her eyes. Rebecca stood up to embrace her, but Genevieve shot her a warning glare and she stopped short.

"Genie, it's not like it seems."

"Oh, it's not? Then please, elaborate. What is as it seems? Why didn't you tell me? Why did you let me go back with my parents and allow them to make me think Paul was my fiancé?" she asked, the undercurrent of anger in her voice rising.

"What could I say to you?" Rebecca said in desperation. "They warned me off. They threatened me and wouldn't let me contact you. I came to your hospital room one day and you were gone. I'm sure you remember that your parents had you protected like Fort Knox. What was I meant to do? It's all very well in hindsight to say I could have done this, or said that differently; but I couldn't just turn round and tell you, 'By the way, my name's Rebecca and I'm your lesbian lover!' You wouldn't have believed me, and I might never have seen you again!"

"Listen to what you're saying, Becca... You think because I lost my memory I would lose sense of my own sexuality? People have woken up from head traumas speaking different languages. What does that make them — the nationality of the language they're speaking, or the person they were before? No one can change who they are inherently, no matter which way they try to dress it up." She squinted, her head pounding.

"Do you remember who attacked you?"

"No, and if I'm honest with you, that's the least of my worries." She stood up, pushing the chair away from her.

"Genie, it sounds a lot easier from your perspective, but... I didn't tell you because I love you and I didn't want to hurt you."

"So you would have let me sleep with Paul last night, 'cause that's how much you love me," she said, feeling her eyes prickling, "and you would have let me marry him, all because you love me. When exactly was it going to end — all these lies?" The outrageousness of how they had all behaved brought her to tears. Rebecca stood up and tried to comfort her again.

"Genie, it sounds unbelievable now, but I really had no choice in the matter. Can't you try and understand that?" Genevieve pushed her away.

"The only thing I understand is that the people who supposedly cared for me abused my trust when I needed them most."

"I'm so sorry Genie," Rebecca said, tears of remorse welling in her eyes.

"It's a little too late for that, Becca." She stared until Rebecca was forced to look away and then quickly walked out of the kitchen.

CHAPTER 23

THE REVELATION THAT Rebecca was her partner and had been part of a deceptive scheme to hide it from her was too much for her to take. Genevieve sat on the train, shaking her head in disbelief. She couldn't wait to hear what her parents had to say about the despicable way they had treated her — and she was utterly disgusted by Paul. *What sort of a sick person would try to have sex with someone he knew didn't want him? Does he have such low self-esteem?* The closer the train edged toward Surrey, the more annoyed she became.

She let herself into her parent's house using her own key and heard muffled voices coming from the kitchen. Upon entering, she saw her parents and Paul huddled over the table together. Paul and her father were deep in conversation. It came as no surprise to her that Paul was there.

Her mother was sitting at the nearest end to the door, and was the first to become aware that Genevieve was there. She touched Eddie on the arm. He looked up and followed her gaze to where Genevieve stood. The atmosphere in the room turned cold, and she felt more of a stranger than ever before. Paul, sitting at the far end, didn't even meet her gaze; he just stared at his hands resting on the table. Her mother sat meekly while her father puffed up his chest. He reminded her of a gorilla, signalling his dominance.

"You've got some explaining to do, young lady," he said, shifting his chair back. The wooden legs made a grating noise.

"I have?" she said incredulously. "Are you joking?" Her eyes darted from one to the other, and confusion spread across their faces. She frowned at her father. "Would you like to explain to me why you have all been lying to me?" She tried to keep the anger from her voice. She didn't know what was generating the heat she could feel — whether it was from outside her body or within. She took her coat off and in one swift movement, not taking her eyes of her father, put it down with her bag on the chair.

"Lying to you about **what** exactly?" he said, looking like one of those jack-the-lad kind of men who oozed confidence and believed they could get away with anything. She gave a short, bitter laugh.

"Oh, where shall we start?" she said. "How about my sexuality. Or maybe Rebecca and Paul."

"I don't know what you're talking about," he said arrogantly, but his eyes betrayed him, flickering for just a second.

"I know the truth, Dad," she snapped. "There's no point trying to lie anymore." She squared off toward the table, standing above them like a prize fighter waiting to commence the first fight. Paul's head shot toward her father, panic in his eyes, but her father sat there calmly, not in the slightest bit fazed.

"And what do you know, Genevieve?" her father said as Paul stood up and appeared ready to flee the room; he looked as pale as a pearl.

"That **he**," she said, stabbing the air toward Paul,

"is not my partner and hasn't been for years."

"You know this how?" he asked, still not moving, his eyes mocking her.

"Because I remember, Dad," she said, staring at him. "Is that it?" she said, shocked. "You don't even feel ashamed of yourselves, do you? Not any of you." She could feel the tears starting to well in the corners of her eyes but was determined not to break down again. Her parents looked at her as if she was mad. "Well, is anyone going to say anything?" she asked, her voice shaking.

Paul spoke first, his face suddenly contorted.

"Everything's about you, isn't it," he said, walking around his chair slowly like a wild animal closing in on its prey. "You couldn't care less about the consequences your actions have on people, so long as you get what you want." He stopped in front of her, looking down on her; his eyes dark and hostile.

"Don't you dare try to turn this round on me, Paul. You lied to me, you all lied to me!" she said frantically, raising her voice. She stepped back from his shadow and overpowering presence. "And you — my own parents. What kind of people are you?" Her voice croaked, but it was full of intensity as she turned to her mother. "What was so wrong with me that you had to lie?" Her mother opened her mouth to speak, but stopped abruptly when she caught sight of her husband's stare.

"That's the problem with women," Paul said, shaking his head. "Always irrational, governed by their emotions. All this 'You lied to me' and 'What kind of people are you?'" he mimicked in a whiny voice. His face suddenly grew serious. "You come into your parents' house and have the audacity to ask them what sort of people they are? Do you know where you have just come from? What kind of perverted lifestyle you've been living?" he asked. "Well," he raised his voice loudly, no longer maintaining the Mr-Nice-Guy façade, "do you?"

Genevieve jumped with the unexpectedness of his outburst. His anger filled the room. Elsie looked at Eddie as if for guidance, but he just continued to watch the pair of them as though it were a show, amusement glowing in his eyes. Her mother looked worried, but Genevieve could do nothing but wait for the next verbal blow.

"You have brought nothing but shame on your family, not to mention making me the laughingstock of the art world. You and that thing, waltzing around without a care in the world — openly displaying your nastiness for everyone to see; it's disgusting. Is it any wonder we lied to you? Tell me who wouldn't, who would want a lesbian as a daughter? A dirty little dyke." He spat the last words in her face.

Genevieve looked at her parents for support against the onslaught of abuse Paul was firing at her, but they said nothing. Her mother looked down and began collecting the tea cups on the table, her submissiveness speaking volumes. *Nothing ever changes there then*, Genevieve thought. Her father had always ruled — he'd probably congratulate Paul if he struck her to keep her in her place.

"Are you actually saying you believe you did the right thing by trying to keep my past from me?" she asked him.

"Yes. Yes, I do," he said and smiled smarmily.

"Well, it didn't work did it? What did you think I was going to do, turn into a heterosexual overnight? Are you that crazy?" She stared at him hard, and felt like she was fighting a losing battle. She had gone there angry at them, wanting a showdown, and in return they had turned the tables on her. Such was her disbelief that for a moment she wondered if a TV presenter was going to jump out of the cupboard and yell, in that annoying way they do, "Only kidding! Of course no one believed they could turn you straight by hiding your past!" followed by a cheesy grin, and "They're not that stupid!" But no one jumped out of the cupboard, and no one told her that this was all just a big, cruel joke.

Her father finally spoke in a voice so calm she hardly recognised it.

"That thing you are with, she turned you into a deviant... She took you away from us. We were only taking you back for your own good." As angry as she was with Rebecca, she didn't believe for one minute that she had been seduced into being a lesbian. If her sexuality had been so easy to change, surely she would have had no problem being intimate with Paul. But she had instinctively disliked any physical contact with him — from the feel of his hands to the texture of his stubble and the coarseness of his hair. When she compared this to Rebecca's attributes, there was no contest. She decided to keep this information back from her father — as far as he was concerned, the devil had led her astray and he was her salvation. Why did parents have children, if only to imprison them with their belief system? She felt like a caged animal at a zoo, longing to be free.

"I appreciate your concern for me, but going about it in this way is wrong," she said tiredly. "You tried four years ago and it didn't work, and it sure as hell isn't going to work this time. You can't mould me into something I'm not — what would be the point of me existing if I lived like that? If I was willing to give up my life and live a lie because you didn't like my sexuality? Is that what you would all want for me, the very people who claim to love me? Would you rather see me imprisoned in your worldview, unhappy, doing what you think is right rather than living my own life?"

"Life doesn't work like that, Genevieve, that's what you're not getting. We have to sacrifice —" but before Eddie could finish his sentence, Genevieve cut him off.

"Just listen to yourself!" She swung round to him. "I'm a lesbian, yet you want me to go against what is inherent in me and lay down with a man as a sacrifice... To who? And to what?" she nearly shrieked, disgusted by the very idea.

"God!" Paul interjected, shouting. "God is who you should sacrifice it for." His face turned red with fury. Genevieve shook her head in disbelief.

"This is all getting a little too weird for me now. You're saying I should sleep with men for God? Can you hear what you're saying to me? Am I the only one that doesn't get this?" she asked, looking at each of them. "How can you ask me to be something that I'm not? How can you ask me to live my life as somebody else, and not be true to myself? That's the equivalent of telling me to gouge my eyes out because they're green when they're supposed to be blue!"

"Don't use silly analogies to worm your way out of this, Genie. You can dress it up any way you want, but it doesn't mean it's right," Paul said, his arms trembling with anger.

"Then we'll just have to agree to disagree."

"So where does that leave us?" Paul said, taking a step closer to her. Genevieve stood in stunned disbelief. *Have I just been talking to myself these past fifteen minutes?* she thought.

"What do you mean, where does this leave us?" she asked.

"We are engaged, if I remember correctly." She sighed deeply, shook her head and addressed them all.

"It leaves us all in a bit of a tangle," she said, slipping her engagement ring off her finger and handing it to Paul. "There will be no wedding and, to be honest, I can't believe you even had the cheek to ask in the first place. I mean, what were you going to say when, sometime down the line, I got my memory back? Did any of you even care to think about the possibility of me remembering?" Genevieve looked at her mother, who had quietly begun to sob. She could only feel pity for her.

"I'm going to get the rest of my things together," she said, not to anyone in particular.

In her room, she flopped down heavily on her bed. She lay on her back, staring at the cracks in the ceiling, tracing where they first began and where they had spread to. She tried to make a picture out of it and when she couldn't, she turned on to her belly and pushed her face deep in to the pillow. The sound of rain beating down on the roof didn't seem as if it was going to stop any time soon. It was strange how rain had such an impact on the way she felt — it made her feel lonely and sad, imagining that someone up in the heavens was crying for all the unfortunate souls of the world.

CHAPTER 24

WITH GENEVIEVE IN her bedroom, the kitchen was silent but for the sound of the rain. Elsie was busy making tea while the two men sat mulling things over in their minds. A final, icy comprehension had spread through him as Genevieve had been talking. He'd realised it was up to him to put a stop to the scattered debris that had littered their lives for too long. The whisper in his mind said, Get rid of the cause, get rid of the problem. At an opportune moment, he'd managed to snatch Genevieve's keys out of her bag when no one was looking. He stood, wearing a smile that he hoped hid his true intentions.

"I'm going for a walk to clear my head," he said, lifting up his jacket from behind the chair. He let himself out the house and walked quickly to his car. Sitting in the driver's seat he let out a deep sigh, clenching his fingers together and cracking his knuckles. Starting the car with a small rev on the accelerator, he put it into gear and steered it away from the pavement, heading toward his final destination: London.

He parked half a mile from the Parliament View apartment block, opened the boot and took a black cap from it. Putting it on his head, he tugged the front down so it shaded his eyes from view. Slamming the boot shut, he locked the doors and made the rest of the journey by foot, keeping his head down each time he passed a stranger. When he reached the apartment block, he peered over the potted plants outside the building and looked through a large window into the reception area. He was grateful to see that the concierge was distracted by two women, presumably residents. He touched the security pad with the blip on the key ring, and without stopping or looking at anyone, walked directly to the lift; he didn't want to draw attention to himself by looking hesitant.

The lift was already on the ground floor. He stepped into the metal box and pressed number ten on the metallic board. The doors closed and the lift began to ascend. Several seconds later, the automated voice informed him he had reached his destination. Wasting no time, he stepped out of the lift and made his way toward the door, swiftly letting himself in. He gently closed the door behind him. The sound of the TV floated throughout the apartment. He walked into the living room, where he found Rebecca sitting on the sofa, her attention frozen on the window. He realised she was watching his reflection. They both remained in position, like pieces on a chess board caught in a stalemate. The atmosphere was hostile, he could feel it emanating from himself and filling the whole room with his hatred. Rebecca's body was rigid.

"Is Genevieve with you?" she asked, buying time, not wanting to accept that he was there solely for her. He walked further into the room, looking menacingly like a cat who'd finally trapped a mouse.

"No."

"What do you want?" she asked, standing up very slowly and turning to face him, taking in his obvious attempt to disguise his face with his cap drawn down.

"To put an end to all of this," he said, expanding his arms.

"And how do you plan to do that?" she asked, fear starting to permeate her body. She didn't want to hear his answer. She knew exactly what his intentions were, but she was desperately trying to figure out what she could do about it. He was blocking the door, her only exit, and the window was not an option.

"If I were to ask you to leave Genevieve alone, would you?" he asked calmly.

"No." There was no point lying to him, regardless of what fate he had in store for her. He wasn't stupid enough to think that she would. "But what difference does it make anyway? You have her exactly where you want her; she doesn't want to be in a relationship with me anymore."

"Don't you fucking use the word relationship as though it is normal," he snarled. Her whole body stiffened. "A relationship is something that human beings have, not fucking animals like you." He began to walk toward her, his eyes ablaze with resentment.

She heard herself yell but it sounded muffled somehow. She felt an agonising pain as he slammed his fist into her head, the force of it knocking her backwards onto the sofa. He watched her fall backwards and went for her again, but despite her dizziness from the blow she somehow managed to heave herself out of his reach and stagger toward the hallway. She was quick and it was only a short distance to the door, but he was already behind her. He grabbed her by the back of her hair and yanked her toward him.

"Oh no you don't," he said, breathless after the short excursion. He began slapping and punching her mercilessly on whatever part of her body was available. When she finally fell to the floor, he began to kick her until she lay lifeless. Each blow he dealt was for all the hurt and humiliation he'd had to endure because of her and her sickness — the sickness that she had tried to pass on to his daughter.

CHAPTER 25

GENEVIEVE WAITED patiently while the concierge retrieved a spare set of keys from the security box for their apartment. She'd reluctantly called Rebecca but there was no answer. She was relieved in a way, because she was still angry with her. She couldn't remember where she'd misplaced her own set, she was sure she'd put them in her bag before she'd left the apartment that day.

The concierge returned, handing her the spare set of keys, and she made her way up to the tenth floor. She was quite pleased with how the evening had turned out in the end. She had stood up to her parents and had set Paul straight about their relationship. Though her father hadn't returned from his walk by the time she'd left, she was sure he now understood that she was going to live her life the way she deemed fit, and she was not going to be bullied like a child.

As she opened the front door, at first her mind chose not to register the disarray of the hallway. Beautiful wall paintings lay torn and broken on their backs. The large lamp, once an elegant show piece, lay on its side with its bulb flickering, adding to the sinister appearance of the scene. She stood there in mute detachment, unable to comprehend what she saw before her. Her brain was only kicked into gear by the sight of what looked like a bedraggled, bloody doll lying between the front room and hallway.

She dropped her bag and ran to the body, putting a finger to Rebecca's throat for a pulse. There was a slight flutter. Before panic could set in, she ran to the phone and called the emergency services, relaying as much information as she could while she tried to deal with her shock. She knelt beside Rebecca again and stroked her face, trying her hardest not to look at her matted, blood-soaked hair. She closed her eyes to the horror of it all. Her head spun — she wanted to be there with Rebecca, but at the same time she wanted to squeeze her eyes shut and block out what was in front of her.

The room spun and she dropped her head onto Rebecca's chest as fragments of memories started to rise. She'd been walking toward the embankment... a male figure with his back to her... the figure turning around. Then, with a force that made her breathless, it was suddenly all there: her father, shouting at her, bullying her, then pleading with her, desperately begging her, and finally, beating her, a forceful blow to her face. The last thing she'd seen before she hit her head and descended into blackness was the expression of bitter hatred on his face.

She snapped her eyes open and looked down at Rebecca as an overwhelming feeling of love rushed through her. There was a quick knock on the door, and not waiting to be asked in, the paramedics rushed to assist. Genevieve stumbled away from Rebecca as they set to work. Her mind was whirling. Everything had come back to her as though it was yesterday. The paramedics were working with some urgency. When they put Rebecca on a stretcher and wheeled her out, Genevieve followed closely behind them.

She called Tia from the hospital, who arrived within fifteen minutes.

"What happened?" Tia asked as she rushed toward Genevieve, sitting in the waiting room looking grief-stricken.

"I don't know. When I went home, I found her in the hallway, unconscious, viciously beaten." Genevieve stared straight ahead, still unable to comprehend what had happened.

"Was there any sign of a break-in?" Tia asked, sitting down next to her.

"No, the door was locked."

"What aren't you telling me, Genevieve?"

"I think the person who attacked Rebecca was the same person who attacked me," she said in a monotone.

"And do you know who attacked you?" Tia asked slowly, as if talking to a child. Genevieve nodded tiredly.

"Who was it?"

"My father."

"Your father?" Tia screeched, jumping up from the chair. Genevieve nodded. She had never felt so drained, so devoid of feeling. Tia sat down beside her, taking her hand in her own.

"What else do you remember?" she asked hopefully.

"Oh, everything," she said, smiling a little.

"Under normal circumstances I would have been over the moon to hear that, but..." She didn't need to finish the sentence. Both women sat there, too stunned to speak anymore.

As soon as Genevieve caught sight of a doctor, she ran up to her.

"Can you tell me any news about Rebecca?"

"Are you family?" the doctor enquired.

"Well no, not really, I'm her partner — she doesn't have any next of kin." The doctor looked at her for several seconds. "Okay," she said finally, "you can see her, but only briefly."

Tia stayed where she was as the doctor led Genevieve into a room off the corridor. Rebecca was bandaged across her head, her face and her eyes swollen, her arm in a cast. She looked like a victim of war.

"Can she hear me?" Genevieve asked.

"Yes, it looks worse than it actually is."

"She's been asking for you," the nurse who was tending her said with a smile. The doctor beckoned for the nurse to leave them alone. Genevieve walked tentatively towards the bed. She took Rebecca's one good hand and held it to her face.

"Becca," she said gently, "Becca." She kissed her hand and saw one swollen eye open very slightly. Rebecca heard Genevieve's voice through the haze.

"Genie?" she croaked in a whisper.

"Yes darling, I'm here." There was silence.

"Did you say darling?"

"Yes," Genevieve said, laughing through her tears. "Don't try to talk, just rest." Rebecca tried to squeeze Genevieve's hand, but couldn't muster up the energy. She felt as though she had fallen off a cliff; every part of her body ached. She had been trying to move to make sure all her limbs were functioning properly. As she lay there in the comfort of the knowledge that Genevieve was back, her thoughts turned to Genevieve's father. *What would possess a man to go as far as he went... to hurt me so badly?* She didn't know if he had been trying to kill her, or merely sending a message.

* * *

Four months had passed since Genevieve's attack, and although the case had been filed, it was still at the forefront of Isabel's mind. If there was one thing that Isabel hated more than violence, it was unsolved crimes. She'd convinced her boss to let her have one more shot at solving it by staging a reconstruction. What had come as a shock to them all was Genevieve's insistence last week on retracing her own steps. Although Rebecca and she were dead set against it, Genevieve was adamant about going through with it, so they had relented and it was arranged to take place the following morning. Isabel and her colleague were working late at the office, making arrangements to set it up.

"I still can't believe that we've had no serious leads from this case," Isabel's colleague Charlie said.

"I know. It's like her attacker just vanished into thin air."

"She still doesn't remember anything?" Charlie asked, pushing his straight dark hair to one side.

"Nope, which makes it all the more frustrating."

"And how are things with her partner?" he asked discreetly.

"What do you mean?" she asked.

"Well, I'm only repeating what I've been told."

He sat on top of her desk.

"And what's that?" she said, leaning back into her chair and crossing her arms defensively.

"Only that you've been seeing quite a lot her. Everyone is talking about how pretty she is, and the fact that you and she are both, well, lesbians," he whispered.

"Charlie, if it wasn't for the fact that you are not only my partner but also my best friend, I would squeeze you by the goolies." He smiled playfully.

"Come on, Izzie, give it up, let a sad man at least have something to go home and dream about." Isabel laughed.

"No Charlie, I'm afraid not. She is very much in love with her girlfriend and I don't think that's going to change anytime soon." She began to busy herself tidying her desk.

"Uh huh," he said teasingly, "so you're just friends?"

"Charlie," she said in a warning tone.

"Okay," he said, standing and holding his hands up in front of him. "But tell me how this works in your world. Rebecca is in love with a woman who remembers nothing about her being a lesbian —"

They were interrupted by the telephone ringing. Isabel picked it up, listened intently and then replaced the handset with vigour.

"I think we're about to find out Charlie-boy," she said with a smile. She stood up, grabbed her jacket from behind her chair and headed toward the door with Charlie trailing behind her.

As Isabel entered the hospital room and saw the extent of Rebecca's injuries, the beginning of tears stung her eyes. Suddenly aware that Genevieve was present, she pulled herself together, trying to swallow the lump that lingered in her throat.

"Hey, Rebecca," Isabel said gently, waiting for a response. Rebecca grunted an acknowledgement. Encouraged, Isabel carried on, "Rebecca I need you to tell me if you know who did this to you." After a few seconds of silence, Rebecca tried to nod her head. Tears were coursing down her face. She was trying to turn toward Genevieve, but the pain seemed too much to bear.

"It's okay," Genevieve told her reassuringly, "you can tell her." After several attempts of trying to say his name, Rebecca finally got it out.

"Eddie Simmons." Isabel wanted to touch her. She wanted to stroke her hair and comfort her, but she couldn't. She understood that that door had been firmly closed and wouldn't be opening again. Not that she believed it had ever been opened, but she had hoped."Okay Rebecca, that's all I need for now," she said gently. She turned and looked at Genevieve. "Do you know where he is?"

Genevieve shook her head, "No — but where do all rats scurry back to?" she said wryly. "He was also the person who attacked me; I remember everything. You make sure you lock him up so he can't hurt anyone else!" Genevieve said as the anger rose within her.

"It was your father," Isabel said in a hush, shaking her head in disbelief. "OK, do you know if your mother is alone at the house?"

Genevieve nodded."They don't have many visitors," she said sadly, recalling that her father's presence had all but stopped anyone from going to the house.

"Do you think your mother knows?"

"No, she'd be the last to find out anything. She only has one purpose in life, and that's to serve him."

"I'm sorry it ended like this," Isabel said sincerely. She hated to see the perpetrator's family suffer. They were just as much victims as the victims themselves. She squeezed Genevieve's shoulder in a show of support and left the room. Walking quickly through the corridors she exited the building and made her way to her car. Charlie was in the driving seat.

"Rebecca confirmed it. It's Eddie Simmons. Let's go." Charlie drove the car slowly out of the car park and increased his speed when he merged into the traffic. The two officers barely spoke; Isabel was locked in a world of her own as she tried to make sense of the evening's events. She had been more than certain that Paul was responsible for attacking Genevieve, and was flabbergasted to have found out that it was in fact the father. He'd shown no signs of guilt, nor appeared in any way nervous when Isabel had called at the house. He was either a psychopath or a very good actor. What he'd put Genevieve through was cruel; but then to nearly beat Rebecca to death? The man had some serious anger issues.

"Well, at least we can put this baby to sleep now," Charlie said, interrupting her thoughts.

"Uh-huh. Charlie, can I ask you a question?"

"Sure," he said, keeping his eyes on the road in front of him.

"I want you to answer me honestly. I promise I

won't be offended." She turned in her seat to look at him.

"No pressure then," he said jokingly.

"You have a daughter right? How would you feel if — when she got older — she told you she was gay?" He was thoughtful for a few moments.

"You want the truth?" he said, looking at her for a second.

"Yes."

"Well, I wouldn't be over the moon — and I'll tell you why. I think you have to be a certain kind of person to carry that burden. I mean, even though it seems like people are more accepting of homosexuality, deep down they're still uncomfortable with it. I think it's because people can't get their heads around it, and that scares them. I would be frightened for my daughter to live in a world where people resent you just for being different and where, if she wasn't strong enough, she would have to live her life in the shadows or might not have a family to share her life with. I don't know, Izzie, I mean, no offence to you, but the thought of my daughter living her life with a cat for comfort scares the living daylights out of me!" She punched him on the arm playfully.

"Hey, you leave Manson out of it, and it's not only lesbians who live alone with their cats, believe it or not," she said.

"Yeah I know," he said grinning, "but a lot of them do." They laughed and fell into a comfortable silence.

* * *

Genevieve's parents' house was dark when they pulled up outside it.

"I'm not looking forward to this," Isabel said, unbuckling her seat belt.

"Would you like me to take care of it alone?"

"No, I don't think he's going to be any trouble. He only seems to pick on defenceless women, and if there's one thing I'm not, it's defenceless." She got out of the car and Charlie followed suit. They walked up the pathway and knocked on the door. After waiting several moments, she banged again. This time the light in the hallway went on.

"Who is it?" Elsie called from inside.

"DC Smith, Mrs Simmons." She heard the rattling of the chain being unlocked and the door slowly opened to reveal Elsie standing in her nightgown, obviously having just woken up.

"What is it? What's happened?" she asked, panic stricken. "Is it Genevieve?"

"No, she's fine, Mrs Simmons. We're here to see your husband." Elsie's face broke into confusion.

"Eddie? Why do you want to see Eddie?"

"Can we come in, Mrs Simmons?" Isabel asked. "Is your husband home?"

"He's in there," she said, pointing to the front room. "What's this about?" she asked again. Isabel looked at Charlie, and they formed a plan in unspoken words. Isabel would go in first, and Charlie would be her backup if he got out of hand. She slowly pushed the door open into the darkened room. In the light coming in from the passage, she could see the outline of his body sitting in a chair. She kept her eyes on his figure while she let her hand search the wall for the light switch and turned it on. His only movement was to put a glass full of whiskey to his mouth, drink deeply, and place it back on the table, empty.

"Mr Simmons," Isabel said authoritatively, moving to stand in front of him. "I'm arresting you for the attempted murder of Genevieve Simmons and Rebecca Sheldon. You do not have to say anything..." She had to raise her voice above Elsie's, who began shouting frantically from the passage as she heard her husband being read his rights.

"What's she talking about? Eddie what have you done? Eddie?" she screamed hysterically. Charlie was blocking her from entering the room.

"Will you stand up?" Isabel said to Eddie, who only sat there impassively. He made no attempt to move and offered no resistance as she went behind him and with a swift movement bent him forward, handcuffing his arms behind him. She grabbed him roughly under his arm and heaved his massive bodyweight off the chair. As they walked into the passage, Elsie ran at him.

"What did you do, Eddie? What did you do?" His facial expression changed from that of impassive to one of disdain.

"Oh shut up, you stupid bitch!" he spat at her.

"Don't you speak like that to me, you hear me," she said, her small hands rolled into fists, pounding on his chest but making no impact at all. "Tell me what you've done," she screamed.

"Take him to the car," Isabel said, gently taking hold of Elsie by her arms and leading her sobbing toward the kitchen. "Can I make you some tea?" Isabel asked, sitting her down.

"No, I just want to know what he's done. What did you mean by what you said?"

"Mrs Simmons, Genevieve's memory has restored itself and she was able to tell us who her perpetrator was." She hesitated. "Also, this evening, your husband attacked Ms Sheldon in her apartment and left her for dead." The colour drained from Elsie's face.

"Is she going to be alright?" she asked unsteadily. Isabel wasn't sure if the question was asked because she was concerned about Rebecca or about what charges would be brought against her husband.

"It seems so."

"This is all my fault," she mumbled to herself. "It's my fault; it's in my blood. I made her this way." Isabel couldn't make sense of what she was saying.

"Is there anyone I can call for you?" Isabel asked.

Elsie kept mumbling, and Isabel suspected that she was practically on the verge of a nervous breakdown. "Is there anyone I can call, Mrs Simmons?" she repeated, but Elsie simply sat there in shock. Isabel went into the front room and poured a little whiskey into the glass Eddie had been drinking from, making her way back to the kitchen with it. She noticed a telephone pad on the table in the passage and picked it up as she walked past. Putting the whiskey in Elsie's hands, she encouraged her to take a sip as she looked up Paul's number in the book and dialled it from her mobile phone. After several rings he answered. She didn't bother with any formalities.

"Paul, this is Isabel. Mr Simmons has been arrested for the attack on Genevieve." She heard him gasp. "As you can imagine, Mrs Simmons is not taking it too well, and I don't really want to leave her alone...." She didn't need to say any more.

"I'm on my way," he said, and the line went dead.

"Why did he do it?" Elsie said to the empty space. "Why would he hurt our little girl? Why?" Tears were streaming down her face. "We never hurt anyone, why couldn't they just leave us alone? If they'd left us alone, this wouldn't have happened." Isabel pulled up a chair in front of Elsie.

"If who had left you alone, Mrs Simmons?"

"People. Why do we live in fear of what people think of us?" She turned her gaze to Isabel focusing on her face. "How many lives are ruined because we don't follow our own paths? How many?" She sipped again at the whiskey, seemingly in a daze. Isabel was relieved when she finally heard footsteps in the passage. She never thought she'd be so pleased to see Paul. He drew Elsie into his arms and let her weep on his shoulder. His face was an open book: confusion, pain, loss — it was there for everyone to see. *He really does care about this family*, Isabel thought.

"What police station are you taking him to?" Paul asked. "I'll arrange a solicitor for him." She told him where they were heading. "All this time you thought it was me, didn't you?" he said to her as he walked her to the front door.

"We aren't clairvoyants, Paul. We do get it wrong sometimes. And I'm sorry when we do." He stopped her and looked at her.

"I really do love Gen, you know. I never stopped. I had this fantasy of becoming a great, successful artist, in the hope that she would love me again someday. I never meant for all this to happen." Isabel looked at him and felt genuine sympathy for the man.

"We can't help who we are, Paul. We can try to be someone else, but at the end of the day, the real you is always the one you end up going to bed with and waking up to. We can't hide behind a mask indefinitely." She walked back to the car and heard the door close behind her.

And in that instant it quietly came to her. Amy wasn't a lesbian any more than Genevieve was straight — but it had taken this case to finally see that. In the same way that Genevieve had to be true to herself, so did Amy. She looked up toward the sky and smiled at her imaginary god.

"Sly boots," she said to him. "You didn't have to put me through all this to make me get the message!" She shook her head at him and got into the car.

CHAPTER 26

THE FOUR WOMEN were sitting on Rebecca and Genevieve's bed laughing.

"And the saddest thing is that Paul really did think he could turn me straight." Genevieve smiled.

"He's one crazy fool," Tia said, mimicking Mr T. The laughing petered out when Isabel's phone rang, and the women looked at her, trying to read her face.

"The jury has gone out to deliberate," she said, her tone serious. "Charlie is going to phone as soon as the verdict comes in; he thinks it will be today." Rebecca gently pulled Genevieve into her arms. She kissed her on top of her head. There was nothing she could say to her that would ease the pain. Her father had been charged with grievous bodily harm for his attack on Genevieve, and with attempted murder for the attack on Rebecca. Genevieve's mum walked through the door carrying a tray of hot chocolate.

"It's like having four children with you lot," she said jovially, before becoming aware of the sombre atmosphere.

"The jury is out, Mum," Genevieve said. Elsie put the tray down on a side cabinet. She had mixed feelings about the news. She'd only seen Eddie once since he was arrested, and she'd realised in that instant what kind of a monster she had dedicated her life to. That he would harm their daughter, and leave her lying on the street like a piece of rubbish...

During her visit, Eddie had accused her of being responsible for the way Genevieve turned out, mocking her for her lack of interest in their lovemaking.

"I wouldn't be surprised if you were one of them yourself," he'd snarled at her. She had just sat there and let him hurl abuse at her.

"Have you finished," she'd asked, eventually. "You are the vilest creature I have ever had the misfortune to meet. You want to talk about our lovemaking? Sometimes your pathetic attempts were so juvenile, I thought the police might arrest me for having sex with a minor. You are just a nobody trying to be a somebody. But this is it, Eddie," she'd said quietly and firmly. "You are what you see every day in the mirror, and it's never going to get any better than that. I hope they lock you up for life and throw away the key." And then she had stood up and turned and walked away, despite his pleading for her to come back. It had taken a long time for her to see how controlling he was, but now it was like she had stepped out from beneath a veil and seen him for what he really was. He'd since written to her non-stop, apologising for his behaviour, and when she didn't reply, he had even sent Paul round to talk to her, but she'd had enough of people trying to control her life. She'd put the house on the market and managed to sell it, despite Eddie's interference. He'd thought that she had needed him, but he couldn't have been further from the truth.

She sat on the edge of the bed and looked at her daughter lovingly. She had so many regrets, but her daughter was not one of them. Genevieve had grown up to be a fighter, a leader — not a follower. She had followed her heart, even against the odds, and Rebecca had stood by her steadfastly, even when she'd thought Genevieve was going to marry Paul. Looking at them both so happy now, Elsie wondered sadly how different her own life could have been. Genevieve mistook her look of sadness as a reflection on Eddie's court case, and went to cuddle her.

"Don't worry, Mum, we'll always be here for you."

"I know love," she said, and stroked her face before changing the subject. "Get your drinks down you, girls, before they get cold."

Some hours later, Isabel's phone rang again. The women braced themselves; they knew this was it.

"Okay Charlie, thanks for letting me know." Isabel shook her head in disgust. The system had let them down. "He got four years. His barrister managed to strike a deal for him, and he got his sentence slashed for agreeing to attend anger-management classes." Though the other women were shocked, Isabel wasn't. It wouldn't have surprised her if he had walked out of the court a free man with no more than a suspended sentence. In her opinion, the courts were a joke and things were becoming worse, especially for women who were the victims of violence. One only had to open a newspaper to see cases of men who were being released and then going on to victimise and sometimes murder the women who had helped them put away.

Genevieve and Rebecca didn't want to think about what his early release would mean for them, or for Elsie. That was a thought for another day. Today they would live in the present. If there was one thing they had all learnt over the past few months, it was that you should never take anything for granted. Life could change in an instant.

CHAPTER 27

ELSIE WAS IN GOOD humour as she busily pulled clothes off the rack, looking for an outfit. Genevieve and Rebecca's civil partnership was taking place the following week and her wardrobe was terribly out of date. She reached for a white blouse at the same time as another customer and laughed.

"I'm sorry," the women said in unison. As their eyes met, the blouse dropped to the floor in their confusion — although they'd both aged, there was instant recognition between them. They said one another's names at the same time, and then both laughed, embarrassed.

"My god, how long has it been?" Nancy said, looking at the woman who'd broken her heart over thirty years ago.

"Long," Elsie laughed, blushing.

"How are you? How have you been?" Nancy enquired.

"Fine, and yourself?" asked Elsie shyly.

"Can't complain," Nancy said, with an easy smile. There was an awkward silence for a few moments before they both began to speak at once.

"You first," Nancy said apologetically.

"I was just going to ask you if you finished your degree?"

"Yes, actually I did, though at another university. Did you ever go back?"

"Oh, no," Elsie replied hurriedly. "I got married and had a child."

"I see," Nancy said, her eyes noting Elsie's ringless finger. "Still married?" she asked raising her eyebrow. Something inside of Elsie wanted to lie and tell her that yes, she was, that it was a wonderful marriage and she had made the right choice all those years ago when she had fled the university in shame, that she had never regretted it or wondered how her life would have turned out if she had been true to herself. She felt vulnerable without the status of marriage — she felt like a failure — but it was slowly becoming easier to tell the truth. She took a deep breath and smiled wryly.

"No, I'm not still married. Did you ever get married?"

"Oh, no," she said, shaking her head. "Surely you haven't forgotten that I'm not exactly a 'traditional' bride?" she said quietly.

"So you're still, you know, that way inclined?" Elsie asked, embarrassed.

"Yes, I'm still 'that way inclined,'" Nancy said with a laugh. "You haven't changed a bit, Elsie," she continued appreciatively. "Have you got time for a drink?" Elsie hesitated. Sometimes she forgot she had no one to answer to anymore.

"Yes, that would be great," she said, her cheeks warming at the thought. Remembering the blouse that now rested at their feet, Nancy bent down and scooped it up,

"It's yours if you want it," she said, holding it in front of her.

"No, it's alright. It's not really suitable for what I

want."

"What's the special occasion then?" Nancy asked quizzically.

"I'll tell you after that drink," Elsie said, tugging Nancy toward the exit.

They sat in a coffee shop a couple of doors down from the clothes shop they had met in. The establishment was empty; the customers preferring to sit outside in the sweltering sun.

"I'm sorry about what I said earlier. About, you know, about whether you were... you know, gay," Elsie whispered.

"Don't be, I'm not ashamed of my sexuality," Nancy said confidently. "Elsie, you don't have to feel ashamed either," she said gently. Elsie's head shot up.

"I'm not ashamed of anything, I'm just not that way inclined," she hissed back at her. Nancy held up her hands.

"Okay, if you want to play it like that," she said smiling.

"Play it like what?" Elsie said, frustrated.

"Look, you're fooling no one but yourself."

"What are you talking about, Nancy? So we had a one-minute rumble. And years ago. Besides which, nothing even happened!"

"Not because you didn't want it to though, Elsie. I often wondered how you'd gotten on over the years. I always imagined you'd marry a strong, silent type who took care of everything." Elsie's face reddened.

"So I'm right?" Nancy said, taking her silence as confirmation. "How long were you married for?" she asked with pity in her eyes.

"Thirty-two years." Nancy let out a whistle. "That's a long time to be in prison," she said softly. What was the point of Elsie denying it anymore? She finally had someone to talk to, and it happened to also be her first, and only, love. Tears welled up in her eyes but she no longer cared who saw her cry. She was sick to death of worrying about what other people thought of her.

"I never stopped loving you, Els," Nancy said to her gently. "No woman I've ever met matched up to you. Which probably explains why I've always put my career before my personal life, and so been a singleton for most of it," she said with a shrug.

"I never forgot about you either," Elsie said painfully. She had lived thirty-two years in darkness. If that wasn't hell, she didn't know what was. She had let her mind be twisted and moulded by others' beliefs, instead of drawing on personal strength to form her own.

"My daughter is getting married," she said quickly, the change of subject quelling the tears.

"I see, so that's the special occasion. Is he a nice man?"

"He's a woman," she said proudly, "and yes, she is very nice." Nancy raised her eyebrows and smiled in surprise.

"I'm very happy to hear that. Talking of happiness..." she said, leaning forward conspiratorially.

"Yes?" Elsie said, leaning to meet her halfway.

"If I recall correctly, the last time I was truly happy, we got rudely interrupted."

"We did indeed," Elsie said, playing along.

"Well, I was wondering..." she said, her voice

trailing off. Elsie felt like an excited schoolgirl.

"Yes?" she said quietly.

"If I were to make you a promise, would you care to help me re-create that moment in time again?" Elsie looked stern.

"That really all depends on the promise." Nancy took her gently by the hand.

"That we'll have no interruptions this time," she said, with a twinkle in her eye. Elsie didn't need to answer. Her smile said it all.

The End

About The Author

JADE WINTERS grew up in London, but always wanted to live by the sea. After many years of living in different parts of the UK, she moved to Dorset with her partner of ten years, where they now live happily with their three cats. One of her ambitions was to write a novel and 143 was borne from the desire to add to the growing genre of lesbian literature.

http://www.jade-winters.com.

Printed in Great Britain
by Amazon.co.uk, Ltd.,
Marston Gate.